HER HEART'S Longing

The Three Sisters - Book Three

BETH E. WESTCOTT

Scrivenings
PRESS
Quench your thirst for story.
www.ScriveningsPress.com

Copyright © 2023 by Beth E. Westcott

Published by Scrivenings Press LLC
15 Lucky Lane
Morrilton, Arkansas 72110
https://ScriveningsPress.com

Printed in the United States of America

Paperback ISBN 978-1-64917-303-4
eBook ISBN 978-1-64917-304-1

Editors: Susan Page Davis and Linda Fulkerson

Cover by Linda Fulkerson, www.bookmarketinggraphics.com

All characters are fictional, and any resemblance to real people, either factual or historical, is purely coincidental.

Family matters, so I'd like to dedicate this book to my four brothers and two sisters. How different life would have been if I'd grown up an only child like Katie. We have our differences, but we pull together when it counts.

ACKNOWLEDGMENTS

Thank you, Air Force Recruiter Sgt. Rich Panagan, for answering my questions about basic training. Also, my brother Harry Martin.

Without the hard work of Linda Fulkerson and other editors at Scrivenings Press, this book would never be.

Katie Mann raised her face to the rays of the September sun and ran her fingers through her copper curls. The cool breeze carried the scent of falling leaves.

The weather reminded her of days when she and her best friends, Haleigh and Aubrey, had kicked at the crunching leaves and jumped in raked piles.

"Katie Mann!"

Is that …? Oh, no! She slowed her steps. She could pretend she didn't hear or see him and turn at the next corner.

Too late!

A broad smile lit his face. "Katie, just the person I was hoping to meet." He stopped and waited for her.

Nathan West. What was he doing in Greenlawn? Nathan had shown up several times last spring, saying he wanted a second chance. This was the first contact she'd had with him in almost four months.

The day's brightness dimmed. She walked a little faster and brushed by him.

"Hi, Nathan. I'm kind of in a hurry, so I don't have time to stop and chat."

He fell into step beside her. "Is it all right if I walk with you? We can talk as we go."

"It's a public sidewalk."

"Are you ready to go out on a date?" Nathan stuffed his hands in his pockets.

Katie shook her head. "I don't think so, Nathan." She needed to nip this in the bud.

"Hear me out before you refuse."

Please leave. She walked faster.

"I've been thinking a lot about you lately." He matched her pace. "About us, actually."

Katie shook her head again. "Not interested." If she was that important to him, where had he been all summer? He'd blown his second chance.

"Let me finish. I know I didn't handle things well back in school. We made a mistake, and I'm sorry. But I want a second chance with you, and I'll do it right this time. I'd like to take you out to dinner on Friday night."

He sounded so confident she would say yes that she resolved to say no. "I'm sorry, but I have a commitment out of town this weekend." She stopped and turned toward him. "We're not school kids anymore. My feelings for you are ... well, I'm not really interested. I've put the past behind me, and I don't want to dredge it up."

The past was the past, and she didn't want to have dinner with him. If she walked faster, maybe he'd get the point.

"I thought you'd forgiven me." He sounded disappointed and accusing at the same time. Just before high school graduation, he'd met her in Pastor Pete's study to apologize to her and tell her he'd become a Christian.

She huffed. "I forgave you a long time ago, but that doesn't obligate me to go out with you." She checked her watch. *Just go away, Nathan.* "We were very young and very foolish when we thought we were in love. It's in the past and done."

Nathan had made himself scarce after she'd told him she was

pregnant. Maybe her father had threatened him, or his parents had kept him away. By the time she returned to Greenlawn after giving birth, his family had moved to another town. Frightened, left to struggle alone with guilt and her decisions concerning the baby, she'd needed a long time to heal from the wounds Nathan's desertion and her own failure inflicted.

"Now that I'm a Christian, maybe God wants us together. I thought you were willing to try again."

The injured expression on his face matched the tone of his voice. She shook her head. Agreeing to date him again had been foolish. This time, she wouldn't give in to his coaxing.

"I've had four months to reconsider what I told you in the spring." He didn't offer to explain his absence or why he hadn't contacted her. "The answer is no."

He rubbed the back of his neck. "Well, how about this? There's a big church in Amblersville that has an awesome drama department." Charming and persistent, he knew how to get her attention. "They do a big production in the spring and fall, as well as a Christmas pageant. The Christmas one last year was fabulous, and I know you'd like to see their play on the life of the apostle Peter."

Peter. She felt a kinship with the apostle who'd failed to stand with Christ during His trial but received His forgiveness and cleansing. She'd experienced the same forgiveness and cleansing.

She'd heard about the drama department at the Amblersville Crossroads Church, but she'd never had the opportunity to see one of their productions. Maybe going out with him once would be okay. Or maybe she was crazy.

"All right." She pictured her father's frown if he found out she'd agreed to a date with Nathan West. She hoped neither her father nor any of his friends saw the two of them walking together.

"Next Friday, then? Will you have that night off?"

She nodded, relieved they'd arrived at the bank, her

destination. He named the time he'd pick her up, suggesting they go out to dinner before seeing the play. She agreed, and he walked away with a smile on his face and a swagger to his step.

Katie arrived home after completing her errands, her insides still churning from her meeting with Nathan.

Should she cancel her date with him?

She'd fight that battle later. Now she needed sleep. Although Katie loved nursing and the elderly residents she cared for, the late shift wasn't her favorite. Sleeping in the middle of the day and staying awake all night was hard, but the residents of the Senior Home needed care 24/7.

First, though, she checked for phone messages. She had three texts—the last from Pastor Pete.

Katie, I had an email about the church drama conference next weekend. Did you register? Today's the last day.

I'm registered and looking forward to it!

As the church drama director, Katie looked forward to the conference. She enjoyed meeting with friends involved in church drama ministry and attending the workshops. She planned to stop at Grandma Whitaker's on the way home from the conference.

When she was sixteen and pregnant, Grandma had taken her in and given her the unconditional love she needed, the love her mother and father couldn't give her at that time. Grandma guided her through her decision to let her baby be adopted, and she homeschooled Katie during her pregnancy. She'd taught her about putting the past behind and finding hope as she looked to the future.

In her bedroom, Katie started to brush her hair but set down her hairbrush and opened her jewelry box. From the bottom, she withdrew a photograph and gazed at it.

"He is so beautiful," she whispered.

She held the toddler's photograph against her chest. The

adoptive parents had sent it to her through their lawyer four years ago. She didn't know his name or where he lived, but she ached to hold him again, even after almost six years.

Sophomore year in high school had begun with promise, but it ended a 'real bummer,' as her friend Aubrey would say. Aubrey nearly died in an auto accident, Haleigh's family moved away, and Katie became pregnant. For a long time, she'd struggled with guilt for her failure, and she feared failing again.

"Maybe I shouldn't keep this. But it's the only thing I have of him."

She hoped she'd meet her biological son one day. He'd be allowed to seek her out when he turned eighteen. If anyone who knew her met him, they'd immediately see the resemblance — the red curls and green eyes, even the smile. She didn't talk about him with other people, except one time with Haleigh Abbott.

The day after she'd given birth, they used the hospital chapel for the brief ceremony when Katie 'gave' her baby to his new parents. Grandma Whitaker and Mom and Dad were with her. Grandma's pastor, Pastor Clay, said a prayer of blessing for the child and his parents. She'd planned this, knew it was the right way. But even now, the memory of that day made her tremble and press her hands over her heart.

"There, Katie, that's enough of that. You have no right to him at all. He belongs with his parents." She tucked the photo back into the box and closed the lid.

Burying her face in her hands, she let the tears flow. "God, someday will You give me another son?"

She pulled a tissue from the box on the bedside stand and blew her nose.

"Maybe I'll always be single. Maybe I'll never be a mother again. Please, help me learn to be content where I am now. You forgave me and have given me the opportunity to begin over. You are so good, God."

WHEN KATIE CAME on duty as the night nurse in her wing of the Senior Home, she greeted aides Angie and Mallie, along with LPN Susan and nursing student Zena. Except for Zena, she'd worked with this team since she was hired.

The residents under her care could move around on their own but had a variety of medical conditions that needed watching. Her shift began when most of them were preparing for bed and ended when they got up in the morning.

The residents in her wing had a hard time settling to sleep. The nurse call board lit up often with calls for help to go to the bathroom. Two residents fell out of bed, neither of them hurt. Because of the lateness of the hour, Katie made a note to call the families before she left work in the morning.

"Katie, Ruth Decker has a fever and a hacking cough. Will you come check her?"

Susan's midnight summons drew Katie away from the computer at the nurses' station. Ruth had complained about not feeling well earlier. It took only a minute for Katie to decide it was time to call the ambulance. She leaned over the old woman.

"Ruth, I'm going to call the ambulance to take you to the hospital. I'll let your son know so he can meet you there."

Susan stayed with Ruth to get her ready while Katie informed the home's night nurse supervisor, who called the ambulance while Katie called Ruth's son.

A couple of residents wanted to get up at three in the morning rather than the usual six. Assured they weren't ill and didn't have to use the bathroom, Katie convinced them to remain in bed. Late in her shift, when she sat at the computer to check records and finish reports, the system balked. The nurse supervisor was able to correct the glitch, but the delay added to her stress.

Despite her love for her work and the residents, when her shift ended in the morning, she was ready to go home.

One more twelve-hour shift and one eight-hour shift this week, then she'd leave for the drama conference at noon on Friday.

Occupied with her work, Katie didn't think about her date with Nathan even once all night. She still had time to cancel, but Nathan wouldn't give up easily. She'd have to somehow convince him that she didn't want a second chance with him.

2

Katie arrived back in Greenlawn on Monday morning, her brain and notebook filled with useful ideas for the church drama program. She called her mother.

"I'm home, Mom. I had a good visit with Grandma, and she sends her love. The conference was spectacular. I can't wait to use some of the ideas they presented."

"I can tell you're excited. I'm glad you can use your talent for drama in church." Mom had been happy when Katie chose a nursing career over acting, but she affirmed Katie's love for drama.

Should she tell her mother about her date with Nathan West? It would trigger Dad's ire if Mom told him, and she probably would. Katie finished her call without mentioning Nathan or the date.

Recalling her father's reaction to her pregnancy, she laid her hand over her heart.

"How could you do this, Katie?" Her father's furious, accusing words had struck her like hammer blows. "What will my clients and the law community think?"

Her busy lawyer father didn't have much time for her back

then. He cared more about his standing in the community and his reputation in the courtroom than about his own daughter. They'd stopped going to church as a family. Mom and Dad argued often and worked a lot. Katie spent too much time as a latchkey kid.

One day she invited Nathan into the house when her parents were both at work, a mistake she'd always regret, and one she never repeated. She'd failed her father and her mother, her friends, and God.

The first time she ever saw her father cry was the day she gave her baby away. After that, he took more time for Mom and her, and they became a real family again.

Although an adult now and living on her own, she couldn't risk Dad's anger if he knew she'd agreed to a date with Nathan.

She didn't tell anyone about it, not even Haleigh.

Should she call Nathan and cancel the date? Going out with him might encourage him to think she wanted a relationship with him even though she'd told him *no*. Was it fair to Nathan?

WHEN THE DAY nurse called in with a family emergency on Friday, Katie agreed to work on her day off. She entered the common room at the Senior Home, and her breath caught. Jackson Stone, seated beside Mary Davis, an elderly resident, looked up. He stood as their eyes connected. She took a deep breath and tried to calm the butterflies in her stomach, determined to maintain a professional demeanor.

"Have you met David's grandson Jackson, Miss Mann?" Mary rested her hand on Jackson's arm.

Jackson's face brightened with a smile, and he stepped toward her. "Katie Mann, I didn't know you worked here."

His smile sent a tingle to her toes. Katie had turned down several dates with him during college. None of her college friends, including Jackson, knew about the baby. She didn't talk about him, and she didn't want to answer questions. She chose group activities with male and female friends rather than personal dates. She hadn't seen Jackson since graduation, and she hadn't thought about him at all.

"Hello, Jackson." His hazel eyes, short, wavy, brown hair, and a smile that lit up his face made her heart race double-time. She tried to remain cool as she handed Mary a small cup containing pills and some water from the tray she carried. "What brings you to Greenlawn?"

"I'm here to visit my grandfather."

"Your grandfather?" She frowned, then smiled. "Oh, Mary said you're David Stone's grandson!" She looked around. "Where is he, by the way?"

Mary's eyes moved from her to Jackson and back. "I see you've met."

"I had the pleasure of meeting Katie in college, and Grandpa went to his room to get some pictures to show us." His face beamed as he turned back to her. "If you have time, maybe you'd like to see them."

"I'm on duty. I'm sorry, I don't have time right now." She'd like many moments to spend with Jackson just then. "But I'll be back to give David his meds."

"I'm disappointed, Katie. I thought you'd come back to see me, but I've been usurped by my grandfather." His wink brought warmth to her face, and the tray she held trembled slightly. Mary watched them, a glint in her eyes and a grin on her lips.

Katie bit her lip to keep from laughing as she moved away.

She worked her way through the group of residents who sat in the common room—some putting together jigsaw puzzles, some playing board games, some watching television, and some just sitting, looking lonely. She had a kind word for each of them, stopping to give an occasional hug or a pat on the shoulder. It was important for them to have someone acknowledge them, and she loved watching their faces brighten.

Several aides circulated among the residents, handing out

drinks. A family with children visited with one woman, and the children interacted with all the residents seated nearby. How they all enjoyed children's visits.

JACKSON SAW SAD, lonely faces light up at Katie's words or touch. Her bright hair lay in a braid down her back, her green eyes sparkled, and her complexion glowed. During college, Jackson had been puzzled by the wall this vibrant young woman put up when he tried to get close to her. Now he had another chance to get to know her better.

"I've known Katie for as long as I've been here." Mary's voice startled him back to awareness. "She used to come with her friends when my friend, Amanda, lived here."

"She really connects with the residents." The more he knew about Katie, the more he wanted to know. She seemed different today, more relaxed and open than she'd ever been with him before. In fact, if he read her correctly, she invited his attention.

"Her mother's a nurse, and her father's a lawyer. Although she used to visit Amanda Abbott, I hadn't seen her for several years. A few months ago, she showed up here as a nurse. And a good one too. She brightens everyone's day."

He could see that. He couldn't pull his eyes away.

"Why don't you ask her out?"

His head swiveled toward the elderly woman. "What?" Warmth crept up his neck to his ears. Had his attraction for Katie been that obvious? "I-I'm not sure I should. And I'm not sure she would go, even if I asked."

Mary tipped her head and gestured with her hand. "She's single, doesn't wear anyone's ring, and she's pretty. I can tell you want to do it, Jackson. I'm just giving you a nudge in the right direction."

Jackson shook his head and groaned. The old woman chuckled.

His grandfather returned and said, "What's the joke? What did I miss?" He sat down in a chair next to Mary, propped his cane against the table, and laid a scrapbook on the surface.

"I'm just giving Jackson some advice about his love life, David." Mary winked at Jackson.

Jackson wished he could leave before he made a complete fool of himself. He caught Katie's eye as she headed back their way with his grandfather's medication. Her smile left him nearly breathless, and his insides vibrated with a nervous tremor.

"If it's about that young, red-headed nurse, Mary, I applaud you. She's a real keeper."

Jackson looked at his grandfather. "What makes you think she'd be interested in me, Grandpa?" Grandpa may be old, but he didn't miss anything.

His grandfather looked from him to the approaching nurse. He opened the scrapbook and said loudly enough for Katie to hear, "Why don't you ask her for a date."

Heat rushed into his face. True, he'd never know if he didn't ask, but what if he asked and she refused?

"Here's your medicine, David." Katie handed the old man a small paper cup with pills and another with water. He downed the pills quickly and handed both cups back to her.

Tongue-tied, Jackson remained quiet. If he spoke, he'd stutter or say something stupid. He felt like a seventh-grader whose *friends* had embarrassed him in front of a girl he liked. It wouldn't matter if he didn't care so much. When she turned questioning eyes toward him, he just shrugged.

The sparkle in Katie's eyes dimmed, and her posture stiffened. If he could only find the right words.

"Do you remember when this picture was taken, Jackson?" his grandfather asked. "You must have been twelve or thirteen."

His thoughts distracted from Katie, Jackson looked at the photograph his grandfather pointed to and nodded. "Yes, we went to the Grand Canyon." He tried to sound interested. It had been a great vacation. "And rode donkeys."

"That was the last year my dear wife could travel, Mary. My son's family went with us."

"My husband and I always wanted to go." Mary sighed. "But we never got there."

"Well, I have work to do. I'll see you later." Katie turned.

Grandpa raised his hand as Katie walked away. Mary nodded, and Jackson managed to squeak out, "Okay." He wanted to ask her for that date, but Katie's expression no longer invited attention.

As the nurse disappeared into the hallway, he tuned out the old people and paced slowly with his hands in his pockets. He'd missed his chance, but he wanted to try again. If he left now, maybe he could find her.

He stopped pacing and spoke to his grandfather. "I think I'll go now, Grandpa. It was good to see you, and you, too, Mrs. Davis." He bent to hug the old man, and he gently squeezed the hand the woman offered.

Grandpa looked up, surprised. "You're going already, Jackson? You usually stay longer. I thought you'd look through this photo album with us."

Jackson shook his head. "I know, but I'll do it next time. I have some things to do." When his grandfather started to get up, he put his hand on the old man's shoulder. "No, you don't have to get up. I'll try to get back to visit you soon. Dad said to tell you he'd be here next week."

"All right, son. Take it easy."

"Sure, Grandpa." Guilt stabbed Jackson when he saw disappointment on his grandfather's face. He loved the old man, and they'd always been close. "Like two peas in a pod," his grandmother used to say. Jackson didn't tell him he hoped for a chance to speak with Katie.

Katie stood in the doorway of one of the rooms down the hall, talking to the occupant. He watched her from a distance, her voice and laughter sounding like music to him, and his belly wobbled. Instead of waiting to speak to her, he turned and escaped out the door and to his dark blue SUV. Leaning back against the seat, he took a deep breath and blew it out.

A water main break had closed school today, so he came to visit Grandpa and discovered Katie Mann. Jackson's gift for teaching and building relationships with his middle school students didn't carry over into building a relationship with Katie. She'd refused to date him before, and he'd messed up his opportunity to ask her again.

As he drove down Main Street, he passed Floral Creations. Maybe he could send Katie a bouquet of flowers. He shook his head. Too soon. He didn't know her home address anyway, and having a bouquet sent to her at work was too public for their relationship, which they didn't have—yet.

Since it was close to noon, he stopped at Hillside Diner for lunch. They had good food, and he needed a little time to work out a plan.

KATIE STAYED busy and tried to avoid thinking about Jackson Stone. She didn't know a lot about him, and she'd misread his interest.

If Jackson had asked her out, she would have ... what? Refused him? Maybe, maybe not. On the other hand, Jackson's interest may have been sincere, and she had shut him out too soon.

Why would she choose to go out with Nathan when so far she'd refused to go out with anyone else? She sighed. Maybe she was just tired of being alone all the time. Was she being fair to Nathan by making him think she wanted a second chance with him? She still had time to cancel their date.

Foolishly opening herself to be hurt by another guy, she kept herself busy so she wouldn't dwell on that hurt.

"Jackson said he knew you in college?"

Her fingers paused over the keyboard, and she looked up

from the computer screen into the twinkling eyes of David Stone. He leaned against the counter.

Katie nodded. "I had some English and history classes with him. The nursing program required summer school, so we finished earlier than the others, but I graduated with him. I still had to take state tests to get licensed, and that took a lot of studying."

"Did you pass at the top of your class?"

"I did okay." She shrugged and smiled. "And now I'm working here."

"And I, for one, am glad you are, Nurse Katie."

"Why, thank you, sir." Such a sweet man. She envisioned Jackson looking just like him in forty or fifty years. "Is there something I can do for you?"

"No, I'm headed back to my room for a while to read. Your shift is about over, and I wanted to say good night before you left."

She chuckled. "It's a little early for *goodnight*, but sweet dreams, David."

"And the same to you, Nurse Katie." He winked as he turned away and headed down the hall.

Resting her chin in her palm, she watched him. What a special man. She loved him like her own grandfather. And Jackson was like him in so many ways.

She left when the next shift nurse came in. Time to get ready for her date with Nathan. Too late to cancel now.

3

atie chose to wear a short-sleeved, golden-yellow knit dress for her Friday date with Nathan. With an empire waist and pin-tucked bodice, the skirt fell just below her knees. She carefully smoothed her curls back into a chignon at the nape of her neck. Small gold teardrops dangled from her earlobes, and bone-colored pumps graced her feet.

She gazed at her reflection in her mirror, satisfied with her appearance. Katie enjoyed dressing up, and she hadn't had many opportunities to do so recently.

Although she looked forward to the play, she still didn't feel entirely right going with Nathan. "If it's doubtful, don't do it," kept popping into her mind, and she pushed the warning down each time.

She didn't want him to see this as any more than a date between friends, but she knew he wanted a significant relationship with her. *Now that I'm a Christian, did you ever think God might want us together?* kept ringing in her ears. She knew her answer to his question, and he wouldn't like it.

Glancing around her apartment, she turned on a light in the living room and picked up her purse and coat that lay on the sofa. She'd wait for him outside.

A blue pickup truck pulled up to the curb. Nathan got out and came around the truck, stopping suddenly when he saw her. His raised eyebrows and open mouth bespoke his surprise.

"I thought you'd be waiting in your apartment." He smiled. "You look nice." He opened the truck door for her. The navy-blue sport jacket and light blue dress shirt he wore with khaki dress pants complimented his coloring.

"Thank you." She climbed into the truck as gracefully as possible, Nathan's hand on her elbow. The interior was new and clean.

Katie took a deep breath and blew it out as she fastened her seatbelt before he opened his door and slid in behind the wheel. He had the radio playing softly, tuned to a country music station. Neither of them seemed to have much to talk about at first.

Katie clasped and unclasped her hands. "You got your truck."

Nathan smiled. "You remembered how much I wanted one." He sighed. "Yeah, she's mine and the bank's." He patted the dashboard. "How's work?"

She didn't want to discuss her job with Nathan. "It keeps me busy. There are good days and not-so-good days."

"Are you sorry you became a nurse? Do you ever think of doing something else?"

"What do you mean?" She frowned. Why did he think she'd want to do anything else?

"You were a pretty good actress."

"That was so long ago, and I was immature." She shook her head. "I have no regrets about my choices, except ..." She bit her lip and looked away, remembering that long-ago day and the little boy who would never call her *Mama*. She still believed adoption had been the right choice for him, but she regretted that she had given in to Nathan's urging rather than saying no to his request for sexual favors.

He glanced at her. "Except ...?"

She turned her face away and closed her eyes, pausing until she could control her emotions. "I chose the right career. I love nursing." She faced him in the dim light. "I can help so many people, and I know I'm where God wants me."

That was close. She'd never make herself that vulnerable to Nathan again. "Acting isn't a career for me. I'd rather use drama as a ministry, which I do at church."

He shrugged. "Well, do you ever want to get out of Greenlawn?"

"It's funny." Katie crossed her ankles. "Most of the kids in my class have moved away. They couldn't wait to get out of Greenlawn." *Like you, Nathan, when you deserted me.*

"I'm content to live here. I have my nursing job, I have a good church, I'm involved in drama, and I have my friends. God has been good to me and has given me a way to use my gifts for Him. But if God has something for me somewhere else, I'd be willing to go."

He glanced at her. "Like if you had a romantic interest?" The corners of his mouth turned up.

Traffic had thickened, and he prepared to make a left turn.

Katie studied his handsome profile for a moment. With wavy black hair, blue eyes, and a ruddy complexion, he was an attractive man. She chose not to respond to his question, not wanting to encourage him or cause an argument. Agreeing to this date had been a mistake. It would be better for them to go back to Greenlawn now.

However, he already had tickets, they were almost there, and he hadn't said or done anything to threaten her. Besides, she wanted to see the play. She quietly watched the passing scenery in the descending darkness.

Dinner with Nathan proved to be more comfortable and pleasant than she expected. She couldn't find fault with his attentive and polite treatment of her. They talked in general terms about their college experiences, and she learned that Nathan hoped one day to own his own real estate business. He had a good job and goals for his life, and he was active in his church. Not once did she feel he would take advantage of her.

The one-thousand-seat church auditorium filled rapidly as time for the opening curtain approached. The lights dimmed, and the audience quieted. The opening scene drew Katie into the drama. She kept her hands carefully folded in her lap as she concentrated on the activity on stage.

"They're good," Katie whispered to Nathan at the end of the first act.

"Told you." His smug look irritated her.

As the story unfolded on stage, she evaluated the scenery, the costumes, and the acting, making a list of ideas in her mind for the drama team at her church. As the curtain closed on the last scene, she'd been so involved in the play, she was shocked to find Nathan sitting beside her. The audience applauded, and the actors took their bows.

Nathan stood and looked down at her, smiling. "You liked?" She avoided his gaze.

"It was wonderful, Nathan. They portrayed Peter so well, and they stayed true to the Bible." She stood and lifted her coat from the back of her seat. "Thank you for inviting me to come with you."

He took the coat from her. "My pleasure." His hands lingered momentarily on her shoulders as he helped her put on her coat. She stepped away from his touch.

As they made their way out of the building amid a crush of people, his hand pressed against the small of her back. She let it stay because of the crowd. Nathan spoke to several people, and she said *hi* to two young men she'd met at the drama conference.

Her heart sank when she saw the length of the reception line. They'd be there forever.

"Do you want to speak to the cast?" Nathan asked. "We have plenty of time."

"No, thank you." She didn't want to prolong her time with him.

Once they were outside, Katie stepped away from his hand,

and they walked, without touching, to his truck in the large parking lot beside the church.

"Want to stop somewhere for coffee?" He started the engine.

Katie shook her head. "No, I don't think so, thank you. It's getting late." The lateness of the hour didn't really matter as much as the company.

"Oh. Okay."

Katie knew she hadn't responded the way he hoped she would, but his disappointed look didn't sway her. Her decision was right, and she wouldn't give him false expectations again.

On the ride home, she chattered about the play. He occasionally commented, but for the most part, he paid attention to the traffic and his driving.

He pulled up in front of the apartment house, opened the door for Katie, and took her hand to help her as she stepped out of the truck. She pulled her hand from his. He walked beside her to the door.

"Thank you for tonight, Nathan. I enjoyed the play." She removed her door key from her purse.

"We'll have to do it again." He stepped closer. She retreated a step. "Maybe we can go to their Christmas play. I'll watch for the dates. In the meantime ..." He looked above her head and then back at her. "How about tomorrow? The state park is still open, so we could hike to the fire tower and pack a lunch. We could light a fire in one of the firepits."

She began shaking her head before he finished. "No, Nathan. You're a good man, and I've enjoyed this evening, but I'm going to be honest. I don't have feelings for you, and I won't pretend I do. I can't go out with you again."

Frowning, he grasped her shoulders. "You know how I feel about you, Katie. Let's give it a little more time to make sure you're sure. You're the love of my life ...."

She put her fingers on his lips. "No, Nathan, I'm not the girl for you. A long time ago, we had an infatuation that got us ... into trouble."

He jerked his face away from her touch, and she dropped her hand to her side. Touching him sent the wrong message, as did agreeing to go to the play with him.

"The girl of your dreams is out there somewhere. Go and find her with God's help. I'll be your friend but nothing else."

He let go of her. "There's someone else, isn't there?" His clipped tone and fisted hands revealed irritation. For the first time, she felt threatened.

She shook her head. "No, Nathan. How I feel about you is just between us. There's no one else. I'm not in love with you, and I don't want a relationship with you."

She hadn't seen Jackson since their surprise meeting at the Senior Home. She was telling Nathan the truth.

He grabbed her arms. "Katie, please ..." She shook her head, and he let go. "You're the girl of my dreams, Katie Mann."

He walked quickly to his truck and drove away. She watched his taillights disappear as he turned the corner. Shaking her head and blowing out a breath, she unlocked the door of the apartment building. Since it was after eight o'clock, the residents needed a key to get in. She made her way upstairs to her apartment.

She hadn't made any promises to Nathan concerning their relationship, and she doubted the sincerity of his declaration. For herself, she felt only relief that she'd refused his offer.

4

*A*s Katie checked charts and began her rounds, she found David Stone in the common room playing checkers with Mary Davis. A small woman with silver-gray hair, Mary reminded Katie of Amanda Abbott, Haleigh's grandmother. The two women had been friends. Of course, Haleigh's grandmother had been friends with everybody.

"Aha! King me, David." Mary pushed her red checker to the last row of squares on his side of the checkerboard.

David chuckled. "Now, where did that checker come from? I was sure I had my eye on all your men."

"I sneaked by when you were telling me about your grandchildren." She grinned, watching with satisfaction as the old man placed a second red checker on top of the other.

He shook his head. "Just goes to show you, I need to keep my mind on the game." His face lit with a big smile. "Why, hello, Nurse Katie."

Katie paused in her distribution of medications to people at a nearby table. "I see you've met your match, David. I don't have to ask who's winning." Mary grinned at her.

"Nurse, I need some help over here!" The call came from a resident seated across the room.

"Okay, Russell, I'm coming." As she walked toward him, she touched the shoulders of several of the other residents, eliciting smiles from them.

Russell had spilled a glass of apple juice on himself, so Katie found an aide to help him. On her way out of the common room, she stopped again to watch the checkers game.

"Do you remember Haleigh Abbott, Mary?" Katie asked.

"Oh, yes." Mary examined the checkers left on the board as she spoke to David. "Amanda Abbott was quite proud of her granddaughter. That little girl had a way with that dog of hers. Brought smiles to many sad faces. I haven't seen her for a long time. I believe her family moved away." She moved a checker. "You should have seen the two of them together, David." She watched his next move with a smile. "That girl and her dog were better therapy than pills or exercise."

He nodded. "Had several dogs myself." Mary jumped his last black checker and removed it from the board, and he threw up his hands in defeat. "You win!"

Katie chuckled. "Good move, Mary! Haleigh's moved back, and—"

"Oh, tell her to come for a visit and bring her dog."

"I'm sorry, Mary." Katie shook her head. "Haleigh doesn't have her dog anymore."

Mary rested her cheek in her hand. "That's a shame. What happened?"

"Sunshine had a tumor, and Haleigh had to have her put to sleep last spring."

Tears sprang to the old woman's eyes. "I'm so sorry."

"She works for the florist on Main Street."

"Oh, wonderful! Amanda had a great love for flowers."

"And she passed that on to her granddaughter."

"I think I've seen the young man who owns the floral shop come in with flowers. Good looking, with reddish-brown hair and nice brown eyes."

"Yes, Will White. His sister Aubrey used to come in with

Haleigh and me to visit." Guilt stabbed Katie. She and Aubrey had been in only a couple of times to see Gram after her stroke, even though Haleigh had asked them to come many times. "Either him or his brother, Jesse. Jesse will be leaving for the Air Force soon, and Willie is going to Africa on a mission trip next month."

"It's hard to keep up with the comings and goings of young people now, isn't it, David?"

He nodded as he finished arranging the checkers on the board. "Must be about time for another visit from Jackson." He winked at Katie. "Ready for another match, Mary?"

Katie's face heated. "I'd better go."

"Tell Amanda's granddaughter to stop in and see me some time." Mary arranged her checkers on the board.

"I will." Katie hurried out of the room. Why did David wink at her when he mentioned Jackson? And why did it make her blush? She knew the answers to both questions.

KATIE CLOSED her Bible and placed it in her briefcase along with copies of the play scripts, satisfied that the Christmas script was ready to give to the drama team tonight.

Even before she had become the drama director at Greenlawn Bible Church, she'd written skits and one-act plays based on Bible themes and people, attempting to make a personal connection with individuals like Adam and Eve, Noah, Abraham and Sarah, King David, the apostles—men and women she had learned about from her earliest years in Sunday school.

These were real people with real problems who committed real sins, not just make-believe characters in make-believe stories. They experienced God's forgiveness because of His mercy and grace. She identified with them.

Three other cars drove into the parking lot right after her.

"Hi, Courtney and Doug. Thanks for coming tonight."

"Wouldn't want to miss it. We both like to act, and we had fun doing the skits during the summer." The couple walked to the door hand in hand and waited while Katie unlocked it.

After them came Chad Young, followed by three young women, Anita, Caitlin, and Lori.

She flipped on the lights. "That new family, the homeschoolers, are interested in joining us, but they couldn't be here tonight. And a few others have expressed interest. I told them to be here next week. But I'll give you the scripts tonight, and we'll go over them and talk about the play."

They arranged chairs in a circle, and Katie handed out the scripts.

"Thank you for coming tonight. Let's read it through, and if you have any ideas or changes you think will improve the play, we'll consider them." The team members always had helpful suggestions. "I'll assign parts for now, but if there's a character you'd like to play, speak up."

"I thought Jesse might be here tonight." Anita spoke, but Caitlin and Lori nodded.

"No." Katie shook her head. "Although Jesse can be quite dramatic, memorizing lines and acting in a play are not his thing. Besides, he'll be in basic training when we perform."

She loved Jesse White like a younger brother, but he couldn't resist teasing and flirting when he had an audience.

"Oh, that's right. I forgot about the Air Force." Anita shrugged.

An hour later, they'd worked through the script. Katie recorded changes and corrected some misspelled words. A good first run-through.

"Good job, everyone. I'll have our full rehearsal schedule set up by next week." Rain pattered against the windows. "The weatherman was right about the rain. Please drive carefully on your way home."

It took only a few minutes for the drama team to straighten up the room they shared with the choir and a Sunday school class. Katie made sure she had her notebooks and extra scripts in her briefcase, and then she flipped off the lights and closed the classroom door. Following the others down the hall to the outside door, she watched as they ran through the downpour to their cars.

The lights in the church parking lot reflected in puddles of water. A gust of wind tore the church door from Katie's hands and slammed it back against the wall. Holding her briefcase against her middle, she pushed the door shut and jiggled the handle to make sure it was locked. The umbrella in the trunk of her car wouldn't help her now.

By the time she reached her car and unlocked it, water dripped from her hair, and her sneakers squeaked from being soaked through. She tossed her briefcase on the passenger's seat, slid in behind the steering wheel, and slammed her door shut against the wind and rain.

Doug and Courtney honked as they drove out.

"Whew!" She rested her head against the steering wheel for a moment to catch her breath before starting the car. With the heat turned on full blast, she looked forward to dry clothes and her warm apartment.

"A night not fit for man nor beast," she muttered as she put her car in gear and drove into the street. She steered around the biggest puddles, glad for light traffic. The weatherman hadn't said anything about heavy rain or flooding.

Hurrying from her parking space to the building, she pulled her keys from her jacket pocket. Her hand on the door handle, a different sound reached her ears. She paused and listened.

Was that a baby crying? Katie jumped when the light from the apartment building reflected off two eyes in the bushes beside the door. A wild animal? Then she recognized the sound.

Bending, she reached down and picked up a bedraggled kitten. Its wet fur matted against its small body, the kitten shivered and mewed piteously.

"You poor thing. You must be lost." Holding the kitten

against her jacket and her briefcase under her other arm, Katie opened the door with her key, fighting a gust of wind. Stepping inside, she held the door until it clicked shut. She scooted up the stairs and into her apartment, slid off her wet sneakers at the door, and set her briefcase down.

Finding an old, clean towel, she wrapped the kitten up, hoping to warm it and dry it at the same time. To her surprise and delight, the kitten purred. Dumping her new winter boots out of their box, she laid the wrapped kitten in the box. She turned up the thermostat a couple of degrees and set the sleeping kitten in the box over the register in the living room.

"What am I going to do with you?" Her rental contract didn't allow pets like dogs and cats, only small, confined pets like goldfish and parakeets.

She hurried to take a warm shower and put on dry clothes.

The tiny kitten sleeping peacefully in the box looked very young. Could it drink milk from a dish or eat regular cat food? She had milk in the refrigerator and a can of tuna in the cupboard. When the kitten woke up, she'd try to feed it.

In the meantime, she called her landlord to tell him the situation. She knew him to be a reasonable person, and she didn't want him to think she was trying to break the rules.

"I don't plan to keep it here," she assured him, wishing she could. "But it's too late to do anything else with it tonight."

"Okay, Katie," he said. "Thank you for calling. It's late, and the weather is miserable. You have until tomorrow night to find another place for it."

After thanking him, she pressed the *End* key. "Now what?"

Sitting on the floor next to the sleeping kitten, she scratched lightly behind a tiny, soft ear. The kitten changed its position, mewed, and began to purr. Katie laughed. "You sweet thing."

She had wanted a kitten when she was a girl, but she stopped asking because her father always said *no*. He didn't like cats. She speed-dialed a number on her phone.

"Hello, Katie."

"Hi, Haleigh, I've got a problem."

"How can I help?"

"I found a kitten."

Haleigh laughed. "A kitten? Where in the world did you find a kitten?"

"When I got home from the drama team meeting tonight, it was in the bushes beside the door. The poor thing looked like a drenched water rat."

"Aw. Is it okay?"

"Well, I brought it in, and it's sleeping in a boot box right now. But I can't keep it."

"Why not?"

"My tenant's contract says I can't have one. So, I was wondering if you'd like to have a kitten to keep you company."

Haleigh didn't answer right away. "I don't think I can, Katie. I'm sorry."

"Oh, okay." Katie tried to keep the disappointment from her voice. Her only other option might be the animal shelter.

Haleigh said, "It's just that I'm going to visit my parents next week. Actually, I'm leaving Saturday morning, and I won't be back until next Saturday."

"But isn't Willie leaving on Monday?"

Haleigh sighed. "Yes, he is. And he said he wants me to leave before he does, so he's sure I go. He thinks I need a vacation, and he's afraid I won't take one if he's not here to make certain I go."

"Maybe he's right." Haleigh had been ill a short time ago. "How are you feeling?"

"I'm okay, except I get tired easily. That's why Willie thinks I need a vacation. I finished my medicine, and my appetite is back." She paused. "I'm sorry I can't help you out. You've been here for me so much lately. Do you think you might find the kitten's owner?"

"I'll try, but I don't know where to start. I think maybe someone didn't want it and dropped it off."

"You'd think a person would be kinder than that and more responsible."

"I know." Katie stroked the sleeping kitten with two fingers.

The kitten stirred. It opened its blue eyes, blinked, and looked around. It focused on Katie. "Mew." It sniffed her hand. "Mew."

"Well, the baby's awake, so I'll see if it can drink some milk or eat some tuna. That's what I have in the house right now." Katie stood and lifted the kitten from the box with one hand and cuddled it against her chest. Its distinct black stripes contrasted with silver fur.

"Okay," Haleigh said. "Oh, Katie, I know your dad doesn't care for animals, but do you think your mom might take it for a few days, at least until you find a home for it?"

"Well, I guess it won't hurt to ask. My dad's more soft-hearted than you might think. And if it's just a few days, maybe. Good suggestion. Thanks, Haleigh."

"If I have any more brilliant ideas, I'll let you know."

"Okay."

Katie clicked off her phone and slid it into her pocket.

She poured milk into a shallow dish and warmed it in the microwave. With soft words and gentle strokes, she lifted the kitten and placed it on the floor. The kitten wobbled on its legs for a moment, took two steps toward the dish, then attacked it hungrily. It sneezed when its nose connected with the milk. Katie laughed as it lapped up most of the milk.

With no litter pan, Katie took the kitten outdoors for a few minutes. The rain had stopped. The tiny thing knew just what to do when she placed it on the ground. Afterward, she slid it into her jacket pocket, where it snuggled down and purred.

Katie walked out to the street, searching for clues as to how the kitten ended up at the apartment house.

A dark blob lay next to the curb.

"Oh, no!" she whispered. A dead kitten, the same size as the one in her pocket, lay in the road. As she viewed the mangled body, tears filled her eyes. She hoped she hadn't hit it on her way home.

Hurrying back to her apartment, she laid the living kitten in the box and tucked the towel around it. She took a clean cloth from a package of cleaning cloths, a can from the recycling bin because she didn't want to use her good spoon to dig in the dirt, and two latex gloves from her cupboard, then she returned outdoors.

With the can, she dug a hole under the bushes beside the building. After wrapping the body tenderly in the cloth, she laid it in the hole. She wiped her eyes with her coat sleeve and shivered, then smoothed dirt over the tiny grave.

How could anyone be so cruel as to desert such defenseless babies? The animal shelter would have taken them. Now what would she do with the living kitten? If she could keep it, she decided she'd name it Chloe.

THE NEXT MORNING, she knocked and opened the back door of her parents' house and entered the kitchen.

"Why, hello, Katie," her dad said. "I didn't expect to see you this early in the morning." He folded his newspaper and laid it on the table as she kissed his cheek.

"Hi, Dad. Is Mom around?"

"What? Can't you talk to me? Boy, I really feel appreciated." Katie knew by his smile he was teasing.

Before her pregnancy crisis, that complaint had often been his mantra to give him an excuse to leave the house in a huff. He hadn't smiled then.

Katie kissed his cheek. "I'd like to talk to both of you." The kitten lay snuggled in her coat pocket.

"Coffee?" he asked as he started to stand.

"I'll get it. Finish your breakfast." She removed a mug from the cupboard and poured coffee into it. She held the carafe out to her father, and he lifted his mug so she could fill it. As she sat across from him, her mother entered the kitchen, dressed in her nurse's uniform.

"I thought I heard your voice, Katie." Mom kissed her. "To what do we owe the pleasure of this visit?"

Katie cleared her throat as her mother sat down. "I hope you think it's a pleasure after I ask you a favor."

"Sounds serious." Dad's forehead wrinkled.

She pushed her mug away. "Last night, when I got home after drama practice, I found an abandoned kitten under the bushes by the door. Evidently, someone had dropped off a couple of kittens they didn't want. One of them had died, but the other one is alive and well."

She drew the purring kitten from her pocket and held it cuddled in her hands so her parents could see it. Blue eyes examined them curiously. "I can't keep her at the apartment, and I don't want to take her to the animal shelter until I see if I can find her a home. So, I was wondering ..." She held her breath as she waited for her father's response.

"What an adorable kitten!" Her mother took it from her and cuddled her. "Isn't she sweet, Tyler?"

Dad's eyes twinkled when he looked at Katie. "I suppose you want us to keep her here for a few days." He reached over and scratched the kitten gently behind the ears and under the chin. The kitten licked his finger, and he chuckled. "Cute little thing."

Katie let out her breath. "You'll keep her for me?"

"We may have to charge room and board."

"I'll buy the food and anything else she needs."

"Your father is joking, Katie. We can afford to pay for her kitten supplies." Mom looked at Dad, and Dad gave a small nod. "I think your father is agreeable."

"Thank you, thank you, thank you." She gave each of them a kiss. "I'll go right out and get the stuff for her." She didn't want to give them an excuse to change their minds. "By the way, I named her Chloe."

"We both have to go to work in a few minutes," her mother reminded her. "You'll have to get her settled."

"That's okay, I'll take her to the pet store with me. I'll get everything she'll needs and get her settled here. I have to work tonight, but I have time right now."

Dad took the kitten from Mom and cuddled her in his arms.

"Uh, Dad, you'll get cat hairs on your suit."

He shrugged. "I have a clothes brush." He lifted the kitten and looked into her eyes. "Hi, Chloe."

Katie watched in wonder, remembering the battles she had with her father while she was growing up. He wouldn't have an animal in the house back then.

He handed the kitten to her, and she placed Chloe back into her pocket. The kitten poked her head out. "See you later." She hurried out the door to her car.

Wow! Dad had been a pushover.

At the pet store, she checked the temptation to buy a lot for the kitten. After all, she'd have Chloe only a little while. She purchased a litter pan and kitty litter, two small dishes for food and water, and a small package of kitten food. Deciding one toy would be all right, she also picked out a small, stuffed mouse, and then added a cat bed to her pile.

After making her purchases at the pet store, she stopped at the Senior Home .

"Mrs. Evans?" She knocked on the open door of the activities director's office.

Mrs. Evans looked up from her desk. "Katie, hello." She raised her eyebrows. "You're not dressed for work, so I assume you have another purpose for paying me a visit."

As Katie approached the desk, she reached into her pocket. "Mrs. Evans, this is Chloe." She cupped the kitten in both hands and held her out toward the older woman. "Chloe was dropped off by my apartment house last night. I'm looking for a permanent home for her."

Mrs. Evans shook her head. "The mister and I have three

cats. We can't take any more." She reached out to rub the kitten between her ears and chuckled. "But she's a cutie."

"No, I'm not asking you to adopt her. She's staying with my parents for now because I can't have a cat in my apartment. I got thinking, and I wondered if it would be possible to bring her in to visit the residents. I remember how they enjoyed Haleigh Abbott's dog. Would it be okay?"

"Yes, I remember Haleigh and Sunshine. I was sorry to learn that Sunshine had to be put down. They were quite a pair." Mrs. Evans let Chloe sniff her fingers. "Well, take her for her shots and make sure she's healthy. We'll have to be sure none of the residents is allergic. There may be some who are afraid or don't like cats." She smiled at Katie. "It doesn't sound like you're going to let her go to another home."

Katie cuddled the kitten, who was purring. "I don't want to. But unless my parents are willing to keep her at their house, I'll have to let Chloe go. Even so, she'll be more adoptable if she's had her shots and health checkup. I'll call for an appointment today."

"I'll check with the administrator and nursing director. When did you want to start?"

"Maybe on my next day off I can bring her in and see how she does. I can't believe anyone won't love her, she's so sweet."

5

Katie chuckled when she walked through her parents' house on Saturday morning. Several new cat toys lay scattered throughout—a small ball, a little stuffed fish, and a stick with a feather attached to the end of a string.

Dad sat in his recliner, reading the newspaper with Chloe in his lap.

"Hi, Dad." He lowered the paper. She kissed his cheek and stroked Chloe's back. "Looks like you have a friend. I see a few new toys lying around."

Her father trailed a finger down the kitten's back. "Chloe and I make a good team. She's company when your mom's at work."

Katie sat on the edge of the sofa. "I didn't think you liked cats. You never let me have one."

"It wasn't so much I didn't like cats, but that I couldn't be bothered with them." He folded the paper and set it aside. "We had cats and dogs when I was growing up."

Katie nodded. She knew that.

"My cat got hit by a car and killed when I was a teenager." He frowned. "I said I'd never have another. It hurt too much to lose it. Between that and our busy schedules, I didn't want any pets around."

He lowered the footrest and leaned toward her with Chloe in his arms. "I'm sorry, Katie. I was quite selfish. Our family life suffered because I was too busy. It took your ... situation to make me set my priorities right. God had a lot of work to do to set me straight."

Katie got up and gave him a hug. "I love you, Dad."

"I know, and I love you too." He kissed her cheek. "Now, as to Chloe, you can consider this her home."

"You mean you want to keep her?" Katie could hardly believe her ears.

He smiled and nodded. "Your mom and I have both become rather attached to her."

"Thank you so much! I've asked people, and I left a notice on the bulletin board at the vet's, but no one seemed interested. Now I don't have to worry." She took a big breath. "Do you think you can give her up for a little while so I can take her to visit the residents at the Senior Home?"

"A therapy cat? Hmm, I like that idea."

"If it's all right with you, and it works out at the home, I'd like to take her in with me to visit on my days off. I've checked with Mrs. Evans, and everything's set for her to visit."

He stood and handed Chloe to her. "I have some work to take care of in my study, so I'll leave her to you. Just be sure to bring her back."

"Sure, Dad." She placed the purring kitten in her coat pocket.

KATIE LEFT the Senior Home a couple of hours later with a very tired kitten sleeping in the crook of her arm. Chloe had been a success. The residents in the common room couldn't get enough of her. They let her go with Katie's promise to bring Chloe in again soon.

"Hi, Katie." Someone called to her as she unlocked her car door. She peered over her shoulder.

Jackson Stone waved from across the parking lot and headed toward her.

His unexpected presence unsettled her, and her stomach wobbled as she waited by her car. She attempted to calm the flutter in her heart and keep her breathing even. "Hi, Jackson."

"I hoped we'd meet again." He grinned. "I usually get here on weekends if I come at all. I haven't visited Grandpa for a couple of weeks, and coming today was a last-minute decision."

"Your grandfather said you hadn't been in for a while. He speaks of you often." She tipped her head. "What do you do, Jackson?"

"Me? Oh, I teach middle school."

"That's right. You were an education major in college. You're rather brave to take on kids that age."

He smiled and shrugged. "You know, the kids have their quirks, but they're not that bad when they know you care. It's a challenge. I suppose taking care of old people is challenging as well."

She nodded and petted Chloe, self-conscious and at a loss for words.

"Who do we have here?" Jackson stroked the kitten with his finger.

Chloe looked up at him with sleepy eyes. "Mew."

He chuckled. "Hello, kitty."

"Her name is Chloe. We just came from visiting in the common room, and Chloe was a sensation." Talking about the kitten returned Katie to her comfort zone.

"Is she yours? She looks quite young."

"I found her outside my apartment house one stormy night. I couldn't keep her with me, and I didn't find another home for her, so my parents and I share her. She lives with them, and I pay for her upkeep."

"If I'd known, I would've taken her."

"You like cats?" Her estimation of Jackson went up a notch.

He nodded. "Cats, dogs, animals in general. On the farm, we've had all kinds."

"You live on a farm?"

"Grandpa Stone was a farmer. My dad inherited the farm, but he doesn't want to be a full-time farmer, so he keeps a few animals and works another job. I don't live there now. I have an apartment near the school where I teach."

Chloe wiggled and tried to get free. "Well, I'd better get Chloe home and feed her." Katie reached for her car door, and Jackson stretched around her to open it. His arm brushed hers, and even through coat layers, she shivered at his touch. "Thank you." She placed the kitten in her pocket. Chloe popped her head out immediately.

Jackson chuckled. "I see she rides in style."

Katie slid into the driver's seat. He stood by the door, holding it open, as though to delay her leaving.

"Not for much longer, I'm afraid. She's growing fast. I'm going to the pet store to get her a carrier later." Katie placed the key in the ignition and smiled up at Jackson. He closed her door and stepped back.

THE AIR HELD a definite chill that October morning, although the sun shone between gray clouds scooting across the azure sky. The leaves on the trees had passed their peak colors, and the wind shook them loose and carried them to the ground. As many leaves were underfoot as remained on the trees.

Several lawns held huge piles of leaves, taking Katie back to her girlhood. What fun she, Haleigh, and Aubrey had raking them up and jumping in them, sometimes joined by the White and Abbott boys. On her next day off, she'd try to make time to rake and bag the leaves for her busy parents if they hadn't hired someone to do it.

Headed to her parents' house to check on Chloe and kitty supplies, she smiled at the thought of her successful lawyer father lying on the floor, playing with the kitten, laughing at her antics.

A hand clutched her shoulder.

"Oh!" She jumped and raised her hand to her chest. A low chuckle immediately identified the hand's owner, and she whirled to face him.

"I guess I haven't lost my touch." Jesse grinned at her.

Katie glared at him with her hands on her hips. "Jesse White, you nearly gave me heart failure!" He laughed, and she broke into a smile. "Some guys just never grow up." She waited for her breathing and heart rate to return to normal.

"Aw, come on, Katie, what would you do without me in your life?"

Tilting her head, she looked at him. "Hmm." She remembered how he plagued the Three Sisters with his teasing when they were kids. The youngest White held a reputation for his crazy sense of humor and relentless teasing. "I can't find the right words at the moment. You do make life more interesting, though."

His teasing grin left his face. "Have time for a cup of coffee and a doughnut? I'll pay."

"Make that a cup of hot chocolate, and I'll agree." Katie needed to sleep after working all night, but Jesse's seriousness made her think he had something on his mind he needed to talk about.

As they settled comfortably at a small table in the café, Katie watched him as he spoke to the waitress. Jesse's dark auburn hair was the same color as his brother Willie's, but his eyes were a lighter brown. Even though he was the youngest boy, he stood taller than either of his brothers. Jesse had earned his pilot's license more than a year ago, and he looked forward to going into the Air Force later this fall. When had he grown up?

"What?" he said when he caught her gazing thoughtfully at him.

"Just thinking. What's up with you?"

"I'm leaving Monday." He rubbed his fingers across the tabletop.

She frowned. "Where are you going?"

"Basic training."

"Oh." She wrinkled her forehead. "I thought you weren't leaving until later this month."

He shook his head. "Uncle Sam wants me now."

The waitress brought their order, and they waited until she left to continue their conversation.

"I'll miss you, Jess." Katie dipped her spoon into the dollop of whipped cream floating on top of the hot chocolate.

"Well, I won't be gone forever." He took a sip of his coffee. "I'll miss you, too, Red."

She smiled. "I haven't been called that since the *J* Brothers moved away." She set down her spoon. "They called Aubrey 'Goldie,' and Haleigh 'Beanie,' and me 'Red.'"

Jesse nodded. "I think Jeremy still calls Aubrey 'Goldie,' but I'm not sure Jason does. No one dares call Haleigh 'Beanie' now." He grinned. "Those were great days, when we were kids. It sure was fun teasing you girls, especially you and Haleigh, because you blushed so easily."

Katie narrowed her eyes at him, then broke into a smile.

Jesse stirred his coffee. "Willie's been on cloud nine since Haleigh came back." He licked his lips. "I've been looking forward to getting out of Greenlawn, but now that it's so close, I feel ... I'm missing everyone already." He took a deep breath and looked away for a moment. "I already feel a little homesick."

She reached across the table and touched his arm. "You'll be fine, Jesse, but I'm sure your family will miss you. Willie really wanted to be here when you left."

He shrugged. "Haleigh reminded me when I told her. But I don't have a choice." He bit into his doughnut, chewed, and swallowed before he spoke again. "You know, it's kind of scary to realize that your life isn't your own anymore. That I'll be told what to do when for the next several years."

Katie lifted her mug. "Several years ago, when my life was spinning out of control ..." she looked at him to see if he followed her meaning. He nodded. "My grandmother reminded me that, as a Christian, my life belongs to the Lord Jesus. I had forgotten this and made some bad choices that changed my life forever."

She shifted her position and bit her lip. It was hard talking about this, but she trusted Jesse understood. "I'm so glad God's love is unconditional. He still loves me. No matter what I've done, no matter where I go, He's still with me."

Jesse finished his doughnut and sat watching her intently.

"Grandma showed me a Bible verse, from the book of Isaiah, Isaiah 41:10. Do you know it?"

He tapped his chin.

"*Fear thou not,*" she began, and he joined her, "*for I am with you; Be not dismayed, for I am your God. I will strengthen you, Yes, I will help you, I will uphold you with my righteous right hand.*" She leaned forward. "Jesse, I've never been where you're going, but I believe God will be with you wherever you go. Ultimately, your life belongs to God. And He promises to give you the strength to do whatever you have to do."

Jesse nodded. "Thanks, Red." His serious demeanor was un-Jesse-like. He looked down and twisted his coffee mug. "Will you, um, write to me when I'm gone? I mean, um, when I can write to you, um, will you write back?"

Why did Jesse act so nervous about such a simple request? "Of course." She tore a paper from a small pad she kept in her purse and wrote on it. "Here's my address and my e-mail."

When she handed it to him, he grasped her hand that held the paper. Shocked, she raised her eyebrows. She couldn't define the look in his eyes, but the intensity of his gaze made her uneasy and wonder about his thoughts. She stared at his hand on hers, then returned her gaze to his face.

He broke eye contact, released her hand, and pulled the paper from it. "Thank you, Katie. You'll never know how much this means to me." Pink stained his cheeks.

When Katie returned to her apartment a little later, Jesse's strange behavior still bothered her. He told her he was apprehensive about leaving, and she supposed that was reason enough for it.

However, when he'd grasped her hand and looked at her, Katie saw a man, not the boy she'd always known. Maybe his time away in the Air Force would help him get over his infatuation with her. Or maybe she'd misread his behavior.

With Jesse leaving on Monday and Willie not due to return until the following week, Katie wondered if she should call Haleigh.

No, she'd wait. Haleigh was at work. She'd call her later, if she had time after she processed her thoughts about Jesse's strange behavior. Now she had to get some sleep before her next shift.

KATIE YAWNED as she unlocked her apartment door on Tuesday morning. What a night at work! In fact, the whole week had been exhausting. She deserved the next two days off.

She'd run her errands later, when it was warmer, after lunch with Haleigh. Jesse had left more than a week ago, and Haleigh expected Willie home yesterday afternoon.

She showered and pulled back the bed covers, almost asleep on her feet.

A knock at the door stopped her. Who would that be at this hour? Grabbing her robe, she put her arms in the sleeves and tied it around her. After checking the peephole, she jerked the door open. "Haleigh! What in the world?"

Haleigh floated through the doorway and spun around. "I couldn't wait to tell you ... to show you. Look!"

She held out her left hand, a diamond ring sparkling on her finger.

Katie grabbed Haleigh's hand. "I knew it! I knew it!" She slapped her hand over her mouth. "I hope we didn't wake up the neighbors," she said in a loud whisper, then drew Haleigh into a hug. Katie shut the door and pulled Haleigh to the sofa, both of them giggling.

"Sorry. If they complain, I'll take the blame. Willie came home, and he proposed last night."

"That was fast. Yesterday you didn't know what time his plane would land, and now you're wearing his ring." She held up her friend's hand and gazed at the ring. "It's beautiful, Haleigh. Have you told your parents yet?"

"I called them after I got home last night. They practically said, 'I told you so.' He got a ride from the airport with a member of his team. He was so tired. He insisted on going out to eat, though I drove. We went to the Hillside. Then he showed me where he's building a house, and he proposed. Afterward, I went in with him to tell his parents, and he was so tired, all he could do was yawn."

Never had Katie seen Haleigh so excited, and never had she heard her talk so fast. She stopped talking only to inhale.

Her friend had taken long enough to discover she loved Willie White, although, since Haleigh's return last May, nearly everyone else knew they belonged together.

Katie laughed and hugged her friend again. "I am so glad for you, Haleigh—you and Willie both."

Haleigh wiggled her ring to catch the diamond's facets in the light. "Honestly, Katie, when I came back to Greenlawn in May, I intended for Willie to remain a good friend only. I had decided I'd never marry."

Katie yawned. "But Willie had other ideas. Let's just say I'm not surprised at all."

Haleigh stood up. "I'd stay to talk longer, but I have to get to work, and you have to get to bed. Are we still on for lunch?"

"You bet. I wouldn't miss it. Two o'clock?" She'd have lunch, then check on Chloe.

"Okay, two o'clock." Haleigh hugged her again. "Thank you for being excited for me."

"What are friends for?" Katie smiled and yawned. "We'll talk wedding plans over lunch." Katie walked her to the door.

Haleigh put up a hand, and they high-fived. Katie was sure she saw clouds under her friend's sneakered feet before she closed the door.

Katie's first crush was Mike White, Aubrey's older brother. Mike, an honor student and all-star athlete, the heartthrob of many girls in Greenlawn, never treated her any differently than he did his own sister. She smiled and shook her head.

Then there was Nathan. He hadn't tried to contact her since the play, and she preferred it that way.

She lay down and pulled the blankets around her. Did God have someone for her, someone who would look at her the way Willie looked at Haleigh, who would make her as happy as Jeremy did Aubrey, whom she could trust to respect, treasure, and love her?

Someone like Jackson Stone? She hadn't seen Jackson for a while, but David talked about him. Would she go on a date with him if he asked?

Sleep claimed her, and she awoke with just enough time to meet Haleigh for lunch.

As she walked to the café, a call on her cell phone changed Katie's plans for the evening. A fellow nurse had a family emergency and asked Katie to work tonight in her place.

After lunch, she quickly completed her errands and returned to her apartment for a little more sleep.

KATIE CHECKED on each resident in her unit, as usual, that night. She knocked on David Stone's door and peeked in.

David lay wide awake, his blanket on the floor and the sheet twisted as though he'd tossed and turned.

"Are you all right, David? You seem a little restless tonight."

David tried to untangle himself. "Just have a lot of things on my mind. My wife and I would celebrate our sixtieth anniversary tomorrow had she lived." The old man's voice trembled, and Katie laid a comforting hand on his shoulder.

She remembered her grandfather's death and how much her grandmother still missed him. "I didn't know, David. I'm sorry. Your wife must have been a lovely person." How difficult it must be to be married for so many years and then lose the person closest to you.

"She was my only love. We met in high school and got married right after I got out of the Army."

Katie straightened the sheet and picked up the blanket, laying it over him and tucking it around him. "Can I get you anything?"

"If you're a praying person, you could pray for me," he murmured.

"I am and I will, David." She patted his shoulder and bowed her head. By the time she left the room, she heard his even breathing as he slept.

Katie hoped David's family would visit again soon. Sadly, some of the residents never had visitors, but someone from his family tried to visit each week. Like Jackson, they came whenever they could. She prayed they'd remember that tomorrow was a significant day for the old man.

Katie hopped out of her car at Floral Creations and went inside to get Haleigh. They had planned a late lunch and a visit to the Senior Home today. Although Haleigh had visited once with Katie, Mary Davis hadn't seen Haleigh's engagement ring yet.

The bell jingled as she opened the shop door.

"Be right with you," Haleigh called from the direction of the office.

Katie heard the murmur of voices. "Okay," she called back.

The shop sparkled. Haleigh had done a lot of cleaning and organizing in the weeks Willie had been gone. Displays of cut flower arrangements, houseplants, and simple gift items sat amid gourds, pumpkins, dried fall arrangements, and potted mums, evidence she and Willie had been busy that morning.

Looking up, Katie watched them through the window into the office. Willie took Haleigh's hand between both of his and kissed it, and she touched his cheek with her fingertips.

Katie turned away quickly. It was sweet and very personal. Happy for both her friends, she sighed. When would it be her turn for love?

"Hi, Katie, I'm ready." Haleigh, followed by Willie, came out of the office. Her cheeks flushed, her eyes sparkled, and Haleigh looked delightfully happy.

"Hey, Willie, it's good to see you back here all safe and sound. I take it you had a good trip." Katie hugged him.

"Hey, yourself, Katie. I'm back, and it's good to see you. The trip was great!" Willie grinned.

"So, I hear congratulations are in order. Well, all I have to say is, it's about time."

"Thank you, Katie." He placed his arm around Haleigh and pulled her close. "The best things in life are worth waiting for."

Katie nodded. Willie White was one of the kindest and most patient young men she knew. He'd waited all those years for Haleigh.

If only she'd waited. What would Jackson think of her if he found out she had given birth at sixteen? Even if he understood she was young and immature, how would he respond when he learned about her past?

"I told Haleigh not to come back in after lunch. She worked hard while I was away. Now she can take some time to have fun and relax."

Haleigh laid her head against his shoulder for a moment. "Thanks, Willie." She stepped away from him and toward Katie. "I don't know about you, but I'm starved. Let's get going before Willie changes his mind or a shopful of customers arrives."

Willie chuckled and returned to his office.

"Okay, girlfriend, let's go!" Katie grabbed Haleigh's hand and pulled her out of the shop, waving to Willie as they stepped out.

HALEIGH HAD WALKED to work that morning, so they both got into Katie's car.

The overcast, chilly day didn't dampen their spirits. Katie enjoyed the light-hearted chatter and laughter she shared with her friend. They bought subs and took them to Haleigh's place to eat so Haleigh could get one of her scrapbooks with pictures of Sunshine and Gram to show Mary Davis. Then they picked up Chloe at Katie's parents' house and drove to the Senior Home.

As usual, David and Mary sat side by side in the common room. Katie loved witnessing growing friendships among the residents, and the two elderly people had become fast friends and companions.

David lifted his hand in greeting when they entered the common room. His smile relieved Katie of her worry about him. Last night he'd been sad, but today he looked relaxed and happy.

"Hello there, Nurse Katie." She leaned over and gave him a hug.

"Oh, and Amanda's granddaughter came too." Mary clapped her hands. "Hello, Haleigh."

Haleigh took the hand Mary held out to her. "Hello, Mrs. Davis." She smiled and laid her cheek against the old woman's. "It's good to see you."

"Mew." Chloe popped her head out of Katie's coat pocket.

David laughed and drew the kitten from the pocket. "Hello there, kitty. Nice to see you too." He set the kitten in his lap and rubbed the top of her head. Mary reached over and stroked the kitten's body. Chloe licked her hand, then curled up on David's lap and purred loudly.

Katie and Haleigh pulled chairs over, hung their coats on the backs of the chairs, and sat near the couple. Haleigh laid the scrapbook on her lap and folded her hands on top.

Katie stroked the kitten. "Chloe's getting so big, she almost doesn't fit in my pocket now. I had to buy a carrier for her."

"We had many cats on the farm." David's eyes held a faraway look. He gently ran his hand over the kitten. "We let only a couple of them in the house. Sam was my favorite, a big black cat with white paws and a white chin." He chuckled. "When I sat in my chair, he'd climb up on my shoulders and curl around my neck like a mink stole. My wife insisted the cats stay off the kitchen counters and table, but she allowed them on the living room furniture."

Mary spotted the book on Haleigh's lap. "Did you bring some pictures, Haleigh?" Her eyes widened when Haleigh opened the book. "Oooo! Is that an engagement ring?"

Haleigh held out her left hand, and Mary took it between her hands. She examined the ring. "It's beautiful. Who's the lucky young man?" She looked up and smiled.

Haleigh blushed. "I think I'm the blessed young woman. Will White is his name."

"Oh, you mean the flower man?"

Haleigh nodded. "He owns Floral Creations, where I work."

"When is your wedding? Have you set a date?"

"Yes, we're getting married early in March, before we get busy at the shop."

"Did you see the ring, David?" Mary held Haleigh's hand up so he could admire it.

"Very nice," he murmured. He sighed. "Today would have been our sixtieth anniversary if my wife had lived." Mary released Haleigh's hand and patted David's.

Haleigh twisted her ring. "Sixty years is a long time. You must have loved her very much."

Katie squeezed his shoulder.

The old man's face brightened. "I had a visit from my family today. My three children and some of the grandchildren came and took me out for lunch."

"I'm so glad, David." Katie patted his shoulder. "I know that means a lot to you."

Katie didn't ask if Jackson had been there, even though she wanted to know. Mary and David meant well, but they wouldn't hesitate to say things that would embarrass either Jackson or Katie if the opportunity arose. She hadn't told Haleigh about Jackson.

The four of them sat around a table so Haleigh could share her pictures. Katie looped her arm through David's and added her comments to Haleigh's explanations. Mary became fully immersed in pictures of her friend, Amanda, but David seemed distracted and kept looking toward the door.

Katie leaned her head toward the old man. "Is something the matter, David?"

"I'm waiting for Jackson. He's supposed to come today."

"He didn't come for lunch with the rest of the family?"

"No, he had school this morning and couldn't come then. But he said he'd be here this afternoon after school."

Katie sat back. David had answered her unasked question. She'd see Jackson after all. Turning her head to hide her smile from the old man, she tried to concentrate on Haleigh's conversation with Mary.

"My brother Jason and his wife Carmella are expecting their first baby soon," Haleigh said. "These are pictures from their wedding."

Hearing a soft step and sensing someone behind her, Katie looked over her shoulder.

Jackson smiled at her. "Am I missing a picture show? Can I see too?"

Her stomach fluttered, and she unlinked her arm from David's.

David grasped his grandson's hand. "I thought you'd never get here. I'm glad you came." David's movement awoke the sleeping Chloe, who opened one eye and mewed.

JACKSON REACHED in front of his grandfather and gently lifted the kitten, his hand brushing Katie's shoulder. She looked up at his touch, and he winked. She blushed.

He scratched behind the kitten's ear. "Hello there, Sleeping Beauty. Sorry we disturbed you." Chloe settled in his arms and purred.

Jackson's eyes met Katie's. "Hello, Nurse Katie." She'd left her hair down today, a riot of soft, copper curls framing her face, and she wasn't wearing her nurse scrubs with a nametag.

Katie pushed back her curls. "Hi, Jackson. It's nice to see you." She sounded breathless, as though she'd been working hard. "Your grandfather's been waiting for you." She wore a pair of blue jeans and an orange, long-sleeved T-shirt. She'd come in on her day off.

"And not only do I get to see Grandpa and Mary, but you and ..." He gestured toward Haleigh.

"Oh, this is my friend, Haleigh Abbott. Haleigh, this is Jackson Stone, David's grandson."

Haleigh looked from Katie to Jackson then held out her hand. "It's nice to meet you, Jackson." Her dark chocolate eyes appraised him as he clasped her hand briefly.

"Same here."

"Haleigh's the granddaughter of my old friend, Amanda Abbott. She's showing us pictures of her grandmother and her therapy dog, Sunshine." Mary pointed to a page as Jackson put his arm around her shoulder and gave her a hug.

He moved over and stood between his grandfather and Mary to get a better view of the pictures. The one they were viewing showed an elderly woman, a younger Haleigh, and a black dog.

"My grandmother helped me train Sunshine." Haleigh ran her finger over the album page. "My dog loved spending time with people in the hospital and nursing home. I used to bring her here."

"And before you say anything, Jackson," Katie said as she held up her hand. "Yes, the dog was black, and yes, her name was Sunshine."

Jackson bit his lip to keep from laughing. Did Katie know him so well that she could read his mind?

Haleigh spoke up, "That's okay, Jackson. A lot of people thought it was odd. You can laugh now." He looked at the smiling face of the petite young woman with brown hair and released his chuckle. "But if you met my dog, she'd make you smile, like sunshine breaking through the clouds."

"I see."

Katie smiled at him, her green eyes sparkling, her gaze inviting his attention. At least, he thought so. He hoped so.

He viewed the photos in between glances at Katie and listened to the conversation as Haleigh turned pages and explained the photos.

"Your brothers are twins?"

"Yes, Jason and Jeremy, the *J* brothers. They're the best, both married."

"Do you have brothers, Katie?" He'd use this opening to learn more about her.

She shook her head. "No, I'm an only child. No brothers, no sisters. Except, when we were kids, I shared Haleigh's brothers and another friend's brothers."

"You've been friends for a long time?"

"We grew up together."

Jackson wished he could read the message they passed to one another with their eyes.

Haleigh nodded. "We grew up together, went to school together, attended the same church until ... my family moved away." Lowering her eyes, she turned a page in her album. She began talking to Mary and Grandpa again.

Jackson wondered what hadn't been said. Katie and Haleigh were both hiding something. Although curious, he didn't have the right to pry. He didn't want Katie to put up the wall again just as she was beginning to feel comfortable around him. If God meant for them to have a relationship, which Jackson wanted, He would take care of it.

"So, Haleigh, do you and Sunshine still work together? I'd like to meet her." He loved animals and had a couple of dogs of his own while growing up.

Her eyes glistened, and she bit her lip. *Oh, no.* He'd asked the wrong question.

She shook her head. "Sunshine is ... I had her put down last spring before I came back to Greenlawn. She had an inoperable tumor." She swallowed and continued. "She became grouchy, and the vet said she was probably in a lot of pain. Walking and eating became difficult for her." She wiped her eyes with the back of her hand.

Grandpa reached over and squeezed the young woman's hand. "Animals can work their way into your heart. Your dog must have been very special. I'm sorry."

"I have good memories." Haleigh laid her hand over her heart. "Sunshine helped me through some hard times in my life." She glanced at Katie again, then smiled. "God has been good to me."

Katie nodded. "I'm so grateful He never leaves us or gives up on us." She took a deep breath. "How about you, Jackson? Do you have brothers and sisters?"

Katie's question didn't register in Jackson's mind right away. What awful thing could Katie have done that would make her think God might give up on her? What hard times had Haleigh been through? She appeared to be quite comfortable talking to his grandfather and Mary.

"Jackson?"

He'd been staring at Haleigh. He pulled his eyes back to Katie and blinked. "Did you ask me something?"

"Well, yes. I asked if you had brothers and sisters." Her voice held an edge of irritation. He had to act quickly before she put the wall up between them again.

He walked over to a chair on Katie's other side and sat down. He could talk to Katie here without the others listening in. "I'm sorry. I ..." he shook his head. The sleeping kitten in his arms stirred, and he stroked her gently. "I have a married big sister and a younger brother and sister."

Leaning her elbows on the table, she pushed a curl behind her ear and rested her chin between her hands. "When Haleigh and my other friend Aubrey complained about their brothers, I told them I wanted six or seven of my own. But my mom and dad had their careers and ... other things. If I ever ... ever have kids, I want more than one. Being an only child is lonely." She sat up and folded her hands on the table.

"I'll bet you had lots of friends, though. And a girl like you probably has many admirers." She lifted her eyes and searched his face. He wanted to touch her hand, but he rubbed his fingers in the kitten's fur instead.

She opened her mouth as though to speak, but she shook her head and lowered her eyes, drawing patterns with her fingers on the tabletop. Then she pulled her hands into her lap and clasped them.

It seemed he'd made a blunder. "I'm sorry. I meant what I said as a compliment."

"I know," she whispered. She stood and lifted Chloe from Jackson's arms. The brush of her fingers sent a tingle up his arm, and he inhaled the sweet scent of her curls.

"Are you ready, Haleigh?" Katie stopped behind her friend. "We have a few more cat lovers to visit before we take Chloe home."

Jackson hoped she'd stay a little longer. He'd missed his chance to ask her for a date. Why did a compliment cause her to withdraw?

Haleigh got up and picked up her photo album. "Sure, Katie. It was nice seeing you again, Mrs. Davis, and you, Mr. Stone." She gave them each a quick hug. "And Jackson, I'm glad to have met you." She looked from Jackson to Katie and back to Jackson and smiled knowingly. "I'm glad to have met you."

"I'm glad to have met you too." Jackson stood, stuffing away his disappointment. He'd learned a great deal more about Katie Mann today and wanted more opportunities to know her better.

"Make sure you keep me up to date on your wedding plans," Mary said to Haleigh.

Jackson started at the word "date." Oh, yes, the diamond ring on Haleigh's left hand probably meant a wedding before many months passed.

"I will." Haleigh kissed Mary's cheek.

Katie stooped to hug Mary and then Grandpa. They both smiled when she did so. "I'll see you both tomorrow night. I'm on duty again."

Jackson remembered how the residents reacted to nurse Katie that first day he'd met her at the Senior Home, as she spoke to them and touched a shoulder or an arm or gave a hug. He warmed as he thought what it might be like to receive a hug from her. He pushed his hands into his pockets.

She'd put up her wall when he tried to compliment her. Was it a shield against bad memories? How had she been hurt, and who was responsible?

"Bye, Jackson." Avoiding his eyes, Katie turned away.

"Until next time." There would be a next time. After all, she worked here, and Grandpa lived here. Unless she purposely avoided him.

He followed Katie with his eyes as she and Haleigh left the room. Where did he stand with her? How could he make his interest clear without offending her? He turned back to his grandfather, relieved to hear the two old people discussing Haleigh's wedding and not staring at him.

He'd come to visit Grandpa today, on the day Grandpa and Grandma would have celebrated their sixtieth anniversary. He didn't want his interest in Katie to be the topic of conversation between Grandpa and Mary.

As Katie and Haleigh exited the common room into the hallway, Haleigh poked her friend with an elbow in her ribs. "Who is Jackson?" she whispered.

Katie tipped her head and stroked the kitten. "Um, he's David Stone's grandson."

"Yes, but there's something going on here. I saw the way he looked at you. He could hardly take his eyes off you. And you blushed nearly the whole time he was there."

"Jackson and I met in college. And we met again when I started working at the Senior Home because he comes to visit his grandfather."

"And ...?"

"The cat's out of the bag." She giggled when she saw the puzzled expression on Haleigh's face. "Okay, let's get our visiting over with, then I'll tell you about Jackson."

Katie didn't have much to tell yet, but she could trust Haleigh to keep a confidence. Talking to her friend about Jackson would take a big load off her chest, and maybe Haleigh could help her get some perspective on her relationship with him.

She didn't want to push him away—she liked him a lot. But if she allowed him closer, could she trust him with her heart?

WHEN KATIE ARRIVED for work the next evening, a dozen red roses stood in a vase at the nurse's station.

She sniffed the bouquet. "Where did the beautiful roses come from?" she asked the two aides there.

They looked at each other and giggled.

Angie, the older one, said, "They're yours, Katie. Someone from Floral Creations delivered them earlier today. Have you been holding out on us? Who's your secret admirer?"

She frowned. Jackson? What was the occasion that he would spend all that money on her for a bouquet of roses? And why send them here, making such a public gesture? No, he wouldn't. And yet...

"Well, are you going to keep us in suspense, or are we going to find out who sent them?" Mally, the younger aide, folded her arms and tapped her foot.

Katie took a deep breath and reached for the card, not knowing whether she should be pleased or embarrassed. She pulled the card out of the envelope.

Katie, you are the love of my life. It was signed, *Nathan.*

Flushing with anger, she tore the card into pieces and threw it in the trashcan. How dare he! She lifted the vase to throw the flowers away.

No, the residents and her co-workers would enjoy the roses, so why waste them? She set the vase down. "Enjoy the flowers, girls. It's all a mistake." She marched away from the desk and put her coat and purse in her locker.

Aware of her coworkers' questioning glances, she began her duties. If she ignored the whole situation, maybe Nathan would go away. He had no right.

Oh, no. What did Haleigh and Willie think? The roses came from Floral Creations.

Jackson hadn't been responsible for embarrassing her by sending the roses to her workplace, but would he ever send her roses—or any flowers?

Katie shook her head. She'd better pay attention to the medications she was portioning out for the residents in her care. She prayed that her mind would stay on her work responsibilities.

7

"Have you chosen a date for your wedding? You said it would probably be in March." Katie and Haleigh waited at the café for their soup and salad lunch orders to arrive.

Haleigh let the waitress set their glasses of ice water with lemon in front of them before responding to Katie's question. "Yes, the second Saturday in March." She grimaced. "Hopefully there won't be a blizzard on that day."

Katie took out her pocket calendar to make note of the day. She didn't intend to miss this wedding. "We'll pray for sunshine and no snow."

"My attendants will wear green, hunter green."

"Of course. Green is your favorite color."

"Willie has some good ideas about flowers that will be available in the spring."

"Maybe you could decorate like a spring garden. A lot of colors will go with green."

"Yes, I know." Haleigh leaned on the table and folded her hands. "And I want you to be my maid of honor. Will you?"

"You want *me* to be your maid of honor?" Katie's vision

blurred, and she wiped her eyes with her fingers. Until six months ago, she and Haleigh hadn't even talked for almost six years.

Haleigh unfolded her hands and laid them, palms up, on the table. "When I returned to Greenlawn last spring, you welcomed me back as your friend, even after the awful things I said to you when the Three Sisters broke up. You have never hesitated to help me. You are the nicest, sweetest, greatest friend I've ever had. I can't think of anyone I'd rather have as my maid of honor."

"I said and did some mean things too. And you forgave me." Katie hadn't defended Haleigh when Nathan picked on her, and she'd neglected their friendship, even when Haleigh was hurting.

Touched deeply by her friend's compliments, Katie leaned forward and clasped Haleigh's hands. "I'd love to be your maid of honor."

The waitress brought their food, and they thanked her.

"I'm going to ask Aubrey and Carmella, and maybe Nancy, to be my bridesmaids. Timmy will make a cute ring bearer, don't you think?" Nancy Morgan, with her son Timmy, lived up the road from Haleigh. Nancy's husband was in the Army, and she was expecting a baby soon. "Of course, my brothers and Willie's brothers will be his attendants, with Jesse as his best man."

"Will Jesse be home for the wedding?"

"We hope so. If not, Mike can do it." Haleigh laid her napkin in her lap.

Katie picked up her fork. "Will you have a flower girl?"

Haleigh frowned. "I'm not sure. Maybe my cousin's little girl. She's about the right age." Her face brightened. "Or maybe Pastor Pete's daughter Eve."

"I like that idea." The pastor's family held a special place in Katie's heart. Pastor Pete and Amy had stood with her through hard times, and their little girl was adorable.

With a pause in their conversation as they ate, Katie worked up the courage to ask Haleigh about the roses. "Did you know Nathan sent me a bouquet of roses?"

Haleigh's eyes widened. "No. When did this happen?"

"Yesterday. When I went into work, there they were for everyone to see. I was so angry. They came from Floral Creations." Her ire resurfaced, but she didn't want Haleigh to think she blamed her.

Haleigh bit her lip and thought for a moment. "Oh! Willie and I both were out on errands for a while yesterday. Willie's new employee must have filled the order and made the delivery. There were a lot of orders yesterday."

"My coworkers could hardly wait to find out who my secret admirer was. I disappointed them, though. When I discovered the flowers were from Nathan, I was furious. I tore up the card and nearly threw the roses away."

Haleigh shook her head. "He doesn't give up, does he? I'm sorry, Katie. If I had known, I could have warned you ahead of time." She sighed and smiled. "They were probably beautiful, though."

"Yes, I left them for my coworkers and the residents to enjoy. It seemed a shame to waste them." She tapped her fingers on the tabletop. "The only reason I brought it up was that I didn't want you or Willie to think—"

Haleigh touched her hand. "That's okay, Katie. I understand." She stood. "I have to get back to work. It would be easy to become careless about going in on time since I'm engaged to the boss, but I don't want to create problems with the other workers or make Willie feel I'm taking advantage."

Katie stood and hugged her friend. "I'm so glad God brought you back into my life, Haleigh."

"Me too. And, Katie, I hope that one day soon, the love of your life will send you roses."

Katie paid for her lunch. *Will Jackson be the one?*

Jackson Stone sat at the table in his small apartment reading student compositions on famous Americans of the nineteenth century, pleased with the research, insights, and writing quality of most of them. The papers, a cooperative effort with the English teacher, Mrs. Branson, included outlines and bibliographies. The students would receive one grade in history and one in English for their efforts.

He set his phone to play classical music. Jackson liked other kinds of music, too, but classical worked best for him when he studied or corrected papers. Nearly finished, he read about Clara Barton, a Civil War nurse and founder of the American Red Cross, as the soft, haunting melody of *Moonlight Sonata* played. The memory of copper curls and green eyes broke his concentration.

He sat back and tapped his green pencil against the top of the table, remembering his last conversation with Katie, wishing he knew more about her, wishing he knew what caused her to suddenly withdraw. Certain of a mutual attraction between them, he knew also that she kept something hidden, something she was afraid for him to know.

He stretched and got up to make himself a cup of herbal tea. He drank coffee for breakfast to get him going for the day, but in the evening, he preferred herbal tea because it wouldn't keep him awake all night.

Puzzled but not discouraged, he determined not to give up on Katie. Tonight, however, he had to get these compositions graded.

On her way to meet Haleigh for lunch, Katie pushed back the curls the breeze blew against her cheek. She'd been thinking a lot about Jackson lately. He popped up in her dreams and in her thoughts as she shopped, cleaned her apartment, or worked. She found herself watching for him along the street, even though he didn't live in Greenlawn.

Her own guilty conscience stood in the way of moving forward in a relationship with Jackson Stone. *I know You forgave me, Father God, for not saying no to Nathan and getting pregnant. You tell us to confess and be forgiven. So why do I still feel so guilty? I feel like I'm still trapped by my past. I'm afraid to allow Jackson to get close. Help me to believe You.*

Everyone thought she had broken free from her past, but Katie knew better.

A blonde woman walked toward her on the other side of the street. Katie recognized Cheryl Nelson, although she walked with her head down and shoulders sagging. Her hair had been carelessly pulled back in a messy bun, a contrast to her usual carefully coiffed style.

Rather than just calling out a greeting, Katie obeyed the urge to cross the street and speak with Cheryl. Checking the traffic, she jogged across. "Hi, Cheryl!" When the young woman looked up, Katie waved. Cheryl's red-rimmed blue eyes with dark smudges underneath expressed such sadness that Katie wanted to enfold her in a hug. Cheryl lowered her eyes and walked around her, but Katie spoke to her anyway.

"Are you all right, Cheryl?"

The blonde took a few more steps, then stopped and turned back toward Katie. "I wish I could die," she said in a hoarse whisper.

"Wh-what?" Was it a call for help? The pallor of her complexion and the gauntness of her face alarmed the nurse. Compassion gripped her. Katie closed the distance between them and laid her hand on Cheryl's arm. Making a quick decision, she said, "Do you want to talk? We can go to my apartment."

Cheryl looked at her for a moment. She shook her head. "I don't want to bother you."

Katie didn't know Cheryl well. A few years younger and not a regular church attender, Cheryl had a circle of friends and a lifestyle that differed from Katie's. Cheryl's sister, Leanna, had been a classmate, and Katie had attended Leanna's funeral after her death in the same accident that nearly killed Aubrey White six years ago.

Katie knew that Cheryl still missed her sister and attended church from time to time, looking for answers to her questions about life and death. She lived with her fiancé, Lars, and they planned to marry soon. Usually friendly and upbeat, she seemed depressed in spirit today.

"Really, it's no trouble. My plans can be easily changed." Katie didn't understand the urgency she felt concerning Cheryl, but she knew God put it there. Haleigh would understand if she missed their lunch date. If she called now, she might reach Haleigh before she left the flower shop.

Cheryl took a deep breath and released it. "Oh, okay." She looked relieved.

She must really need to talk to agree so readily. Katie pulled out her phone. "I have to make one call." She speed-dialed Haleigh's number. "Hi. Um, something has come up, and I won't make it for lunch .... No, I'm okay. Talk to you later." She closed her phone and pocketed it. "Okay. My apartment's this way."

Cheryl didn't keep up her usual chatter, and Katie tried to fill in the quiet with an occasional comment about the weather, a flower garden, and Chloe. She smiled at Katie's description of the kitten's antics. Too bad Chloe lived with her parents and not at her apartment. If Cheryl liked cats, and Katie surmised she did, the kitten could soothe the young woman's troubled spirit.

Katie unlocked her door and invited Cheryl into her apartment. She took off her jacket. "May I take your coat?"

Cheryl shook her head as she gazed around Katie's comfortable home. "This is nice. Your apartment is both cozy and well-coordinated. Did you decorate yourself?"

"Yes. I had a lot of fun doing it."

"I know what you mean. That's why I chose interior decorating as a career. Putting together colors, textures, and styles to create a home is rewarding."

"That's right, you're an interior decorator. How is your business doing?" Katie indicated the comfortable recliner for her guest to sit in.

"Very well, thank you." Cheryl perched on the edge of the chair, her fingers tapping against the arms.

"Can I get you something to eat or drink? Have you had lunch yet?"

Cheryl shook her head. "I-I'm not really hungry, but a drink would be appreciated."

"A cup of tea? Water?"

"Tea sounds wonderful. Do you have any herbal teas?"

"Peppermint, chamomile, berry, orange-spice, lemon."

"Peppermint, please."

Katie boiled water in the tea kettle and brewed two mugs of peppermint tea. She set them on a tray with sugar and milk and placed the tray on her coffee table.

"If you care for sugar or milk in your tea, help yourself." Katie sat on the sofa.

"Thank you. I prefer it plain." Cheryl picked up a mug. "I like the sunflower pattern on your mugs. Lars and I saw some ...." She bit her lip and held the mug between trembling hands. She breathed in the steam from her tea and blew on it. "I like herbal tea plain, especially the peppermint."

She set the mug on a coaster. "I suppose you're wondering why I said what I did earlier. About dying."

Katie nodded and waited silently. It would be best to let Cheryl speak before asking any questions.

The young woman licked her lips and pushed some strands of hair behind her ears. "Lars and I ..." She choked on her words and lifted her mug to take a sip. She set the mug down and breathed deeply. "I'm pregnant."

Katie's mouth rounded into an *O*. A sense of *déjà vu* coursed through her. Her own breath shortened, and her heart beat harder as she processed Cheryl's words.

Tears filled Cheryl's eyes. She got up. "So now you know. Thanks for the tea. I'll be going."

Katie stood quickly, whispering a prayer for help. She laid her hand on Cheryl's shoulder. "Please sit down. You haven't finished your tea."

"No, my coming here was a mistake. You're a good Christian. You wouldn't understand."

Katie stepped in front of Cheryl and said softly, "But I do." Cheryl made eye contact. "I do understand. More than you think."

After a moment, Cheryl nodded once and sat down again. Katie returned to the sofa.

"How ... how does Lars feel about it?"

Cheryl shook her head. "We took precautions. We didn't plan to start a family until a few years after getting married. I was excited at first when I found out. After all, having a baby is what women do. But when I told Lars, he ... he said to get rid of it."

"Oh, Cheryl." That had been Katie's father's reaction to her pregnancy. He'd wanted to set up an abortion for her immediately. Getting off the sofa, she knelt in front of Cheryl and took both her hands. "You probably didn't know, and most people don't remember, but almost six years ago, after Leanna died, I had a baby." Katie's hands shook and her insides quivered. She waited for Cheryl's reaction.

Cheryl's jaw dropped. "But you ... but I ..." She leaned forward. "What did you do?"

Katie shook her head. "My dad went ballistic. He demanded that I have an abortion right away, although he changed his mind later. Babies aren't garbage that we throw away. They're not just tissue. They're human beings, made in God's image, with a right to life. With my grandmother's help, and my mom's, I gave birth to the baby and gave him up for adoption."

"But why ...?" Cheryl pulled her hands away. "I didn't know." She bit her lip. "Was it that Nathan West guy?" Katie's relationship with Nathan hadn't been a secret. Cheryl must have seen them together, even as a younger student.

"Yes." Katie returned to the sofa. "Nathan's family left town after I told him. I lived with my grandmother, away from Greenlawn, until after the baby's birth. Giving up my baby was the hardest thing I ever had to do." Her voice thickened, and she swallowed a sob. "But it was the right thing."

Cheryl picked up her mug and took several sips of tea. Katie did the same, the silence in the apartment broken only by the sounds of the refrigerator, cars passing by on the street, and a downstairs door slamming.

Cheryl frowned. "But you were only a teenager, and I'm an adult. I'm not sure I can go through an entire pregnancy and give my baby to someone else."

"Would you be able to keep it yourself?" The choice had to be Cheryl's. Katie couldn't tell her what to do.

Cheryl stood and walked to the window. She pulled aside the curtain and looked out. She turned back to Katie and shook her head. "Lars said if I don't have an abortion, he'll leave. I can't live without Lars." She covered her face with her hands and sobbed.

Katie's heart broke, and she gathered Cheryl into her arms. "Father God, Cheryl is hurting so much right now. Help her to know you love her and care about her. And you care about the baby and Lars. Help her in the decisions she must make. In Jesus' name."

After a couple of minutes, Cheryl stopped sobbing and stepped back from Katie's embrace. She took a handful of tissues from the box Katie offered her to wipe her face and blow her nose. She sat, leaned back, and closed her eyes.

Katie returned the box to the coffee table. "I have something." She stepped over to her bookshelf and pulled off a small book. Returning to the sofa, she ran her hand over the book's cover.

"I wouldn't have been able to get through without Jesus' help." She pushed a curl behind her ear and stared at the book cover. "I failed God when I didn't say no to Nathan. The Bible says that kind of relationship should take place only between a man and a woman married to each other." She paused, choosing her words carefully so as not to turn the other woman off.

"I received Jesus as my Savior as a child. I knew allowing my relationship with Nathan to become intimate was wrong. But I chose to sin, to disobey God's Word." She glanced at Cheryl to find her watching her closely. "I confessed my sin, and He forgave me. He gave me a second chance."

She took a deep breath. "I know you come to church sometimes, but I don't know whether you have a personal relationship with Jesus Christ. He loves you so much, Cheryl, that He died on the cross to pay for your sin. He wants to be your Savior and help you, too, if you'll let Him."

Cheryl finished her tea and set down her mug, and Katie waited for her to speak.

"I never understood why God let Leanna die. But I know why I'm pregnant. Lars and I are so in love, living together seems right." She bit her lip and shook her head. "I don't think I'm ready for what you call a personal relationship with Jesus Christ."

"My grandmother gave me this book. There's a short reading and a few Bible verses for each day. It helped me to understand more about who God is and God's love and forgiveness." She held the book out to Cheryl. "I'll let you take it, if you want."

Cheryl hesitated, then reached out and took the book. She flipped through it. "Okay, I'll try. Thanks."

At least Cheryl hadn't rejected her offering. "Another thing that helped me was talking to the pastor. Pastor Pete ... well, you know him. You could call and set up a time to talk with him. I can give you his number."

Cheryl nodded, and Katie wrote down Pastor Pete's telephone number and added her own.

The troubled young woman stood up. "I should be going now." She shrugged into her coat. She glanced at the piece of paper Katie handed her and stuffed it in her coat pocket. At the door she turned to Katie. "And thanks."

Katie laid her hand on Cheryl's arm. "If you need to talk again, you know how to get in touch with me. And I'll be praying." She opened the door.

Head up and shoulders back, Cheryl strode to the stairs and down, never looking back.

As she closed her door, Katie shook her head. She recognized the false bravado in Cheryl's attitude. The wounded young woman faced some tough decisions, and Katie didn't know if she would choose life for her baby. Even though she wanted the baby, she wanted Lars too.

Katie's own choice had been based on her Christian belief in the sanctity of life as created by God. Cheryl wasn't a Christian. She would feel pressure from people who considered abortion a convenient choice.

Katie picked up her phone to call Haleigh and ask her to pray for Cheryl, but she set the phone down. What Cheryl had told her was confidential, her own secret to share if and with whom she wanted to tell it. Instead, Katie knelt by the sofa and poured out her heart in prayer for Cheryl, Lars, and the important decisions they had to make. She prayed that they both would be saved, and that they would choose life for their baby.

Her stomach growled, reminding her she had missed lunch. As she ate a bowl of chicken and rice soup, the thought about how quickly God had responded to her earlier prayer nearly took her breath away. In speaking the truth to Cheryl, she'd finally broken through a wall that had kept her trapped for so long.

Yes, she'd sinned. But it was also true that she was completely forgiven and didn't have to hide. She knew there were other young women who might benefit from her honesty.

In the busyness of her life, she'd set aside the idea of helping with a crisis pregnancy hotline. She'd call Grandma Whitman for information. Maybe Haleigh would be interested in becoming a hotline counselor along with her.

8

On the way to her car after play practice, Katie's phone vibrated. She dug it out of her coat pocket and read the screen, then clicked it on. "Hi, Haleigh."

"Guess what? Carmella and Jason are at the hospital. My mom just called." She sounded breathless, excited.

"Oh, Haleigh, that's wonderful!" Haleigh's brother had been her friend for a long time, like her own brother, and would soon become a father. She shared Haleigh's excitement.

"Yes. I hoped the baby might wait for another week and be born on my birthday, but then I guess every baby deserves its own birthday." She giggled. "I think Mexican jumping beans are having a party in my stomach."

Katie unlocked her car and got in. "I guess you'll know soon enough whether you have a niece or a nephew." She started her car and turned up the heater.

"I can't believe they could wait to find out themselves."

"Well, maybe they know. Maybe they couldn't wait to find out but didn't tell anyone else."

"Well, I suppose. But I made an outfit for a boy and one for a girl." Haleigh sighed. "Willie and I are going to see them Saturday. Do you want to go with us?"

The memory of a little boy with red curls and green eyes shadowed her happiness for her friend. She shivered, but not from the cold.

"I'd love to see the new baby, but I have to work Saturday. I appreciate the invitation." Haleigh and Willie would probably prefer the time alone anyway. "Maybe they'll come to Greenlawn sometime soon."

"They probably will. I'll be sure to invite them." Haleigh paused. "I missed you at lunch. Is everything okay?"

"I'm fine." Katie nibbled her bottom lip. How much should she say? "Someone had ... a problem, and I felt a strong inner urge to help." She adjusted the heat. "I can't tell you much, but will you pray for this person?"

"Of course. I'm curious, but I don't have to know any more. God knows."

Katie knew Haleigh and Willie prayed for Cheryl and Lars, and their hearts would be as heavy as hers if they knew the situation. Although she trusted her friend to keep a confidence, Cheryl should be the one to tell Haleigh.

"We had play practice tonight. Everyone loves the costumes. You and Mrs. Hayes did a fabulous job making them."

"Thanks, Katie. Mrs. Hayes works magic with her needle. I've learned so much from her." Haleigh yawned. "Willie just brought me back to my house. We had dinner with his parents tonight."

"Any news from Jesse?"

"They got a package with his clothes in the mail. It may be a while before he's allowed to call home. Mrs. White doesn't say much, but she misses him terribly."

"I'm sure the house is very quiet without him." Katie hadn't received a letter from Jesse yet. "At least Mrs. White still has Willie at home for now."

"Jeremy and Aubrey are planning to come to Greenlawn for Thanksgiving, and Mike and Madison will be here too. Willie and I plan to spend Christmas in Wellsburg with my family, since

Carmella and the baby should be fine for travel by then. The Whites will get together again on New Year's Day."

"I volunteered to work Thanksgiving Day so the nurse with a family could have the day off. Grandma Whitman and my aunt and uncle and cousins are coming here for Thanksgiving, so I'll at least get to see them for a little while after work."

"That's good," Haleigh said.

"It is. I haven't seen my cousins for a long time. Some of them are married now. I'm not sure about Christmas yet. I think my parents want to invite my dad's family to come to their house."

"Are we still on for lunch tomorrow?"

"Certainly. I wouldn't want to stand up my best friend twice in a row."

"Well, you had a good reason, so you're forgiven for missing yesterday. I'll let you know when I hear something more about Carmella and the baby."

"It may be a while. First babies often take their time arriving." Katie had spent rotations in the delivery room during nurse's training. What she remembered most about her own birth experience wasn't the delivery but the day after, when she left the hospital with empty arms. "I'll make sure my phone is charged, so I won't miss your call."

"Okay. Good night, Katie."

"Bye, Haleigh." Katie closed her phone and immediately prayed for Carmella, the baby, and the Abbott family.

She paused for a moment in her prayer, then added, "Father in heaven, please allow me to be a mother one day and raise my child. If Jackson is the right man for me, give me the courage to be honest with him. And God, please help Cheryl to make the right decision, and let Lars love her so much that he'll do the right thing by her. They both need Jesus as Savior. I pray that they'll both say "yes" to You. In Jesus' name, Amen."

Good thing she didn't have a long drive home. She had trouble keeping her mind on driving.

IN THE MORNING, she had a message on her phone, a photo of a newborn with the inscription Jonathan Luke Abbott.

"Thank you for this new life, Father," she whispered.

He's beautiful. Congratulations, Aunt Haleigh!

About nine, when she was ready to visit her parents and Chloe, her phone rang.

"Hi, Haleigh. How are the baby and his parents?"

"Katie," Haleigh choked out.

"What's wrong?"

"Carmella was hemorrhaging. They had a hard time stopping it."

"Oh, Haleigh." As a nurse, she understood the threat to Carmella's life, and Haleigh had struggled so with losses in the past. "Let me pray with you." She didn't wait for Haleigh's approval but immediately prayed for Carmella, Jason, and the baby.

Haleigh took a deep breath and exhaled. "Thank you, Katie. I shouldn't have panicked."

"She'll probably be okay because they treated it right away. Is the baby all right?"

"He seems to be. My mother says he has a great set of lungs." She gave a quick laugh. "I'm glad Mom and Dad are there for them. And Carmella's parents too."

Katie checked the time. "Are you at home or at work?"

"I'm at work. I have to keep busy so I don't think too much, and there's a lot to do here."

"Well, if you feel you can't meet me for lunch, just let me know. I'm going over to take care of Chloe now, but I'll have my phone with me."

"Okay. Thanks, Katie. What would I do without you?"

"Miss me, not be able to call me in an emergency, not have anyone to go to lunch with ... except Willie ...."

"Okay, okay, I get the picture." They both laughed. "Bye, Katie."

"Talk to you later." Katie ended the call and put the phone in her pocket.

By taking the car rather than walking, she could stop at Floral Creations later to check up on Haleigh and get the current news in person.

Finding neither of her parents at home, she cleaned the litter pan, checked cat supplies, and left a note for her parents to inform them of Jonathan's birth and Carmella's need for prayer. She tucked Chloe into her coat pocket. Instead of curling up inside, the kitten poked her head out and looked about with bright eyes. Katie scratched behind Chloe's ears before drawing on her gloves.

"The carrier's in the car, Chloe. I don't want you jumping out of my pocket and getting away from me."

"Mew." Chloe blinked at Katie. She rested her front paws on the edge of the pocket and purred.

The bell on the door at Floral Creations jingled as she opened it. Several customers browsed. Haleigh spoke to someone on her cell phone. She held up her index finger and mouthed, *Just a minute.* Tia helped a customer at the cash register.

Haleigh closed her cell phone with a smile. "Carmella's okay. She's sleeping now, and the baby's okay." She turned to one of the customers. "May I help you?"

"Look, Mommy, that lady has a kitty in her pocket." A little girl tugged on her mother's coat. She pulled the woman's attention from the spider plant she was examining to Chloe peeking out at them.

Katie often brought Chloe into Floral Creations with her, and today was too cold to leave her in the car.

The mother smiled and nodded. "A pretty kitten too."

Katie squatted down next to the girl, who clung shyly to her mother's coat and took Chloe out of her pocket. The kitten blinked at the girl. "Her name is Chloe."

The girl's blue eyes grew big. "That's my name too."

Katie chuckled. "Chloe, meet Chloe. She likes people." She held the kitten out. "You may pet her if your mommy says it's all right."

The girl looked up, and her mother nodded. She gently touched Chloe's head. The kitten sniffed her hand. "Mew."

The girl Chloe giggled and stroked the kitten's back. "She's so soft."

"Her fur has such an interesting pattern," the mother said.

"Yes, and she has blue eyes like your daughter."

The little girl sighed. "I wish I could have a kitten."

"Maybe one day, honey." The mom turned to Katie. "Did you buy her from a pet store?"

Katie shook her head. "No. Someone abandoned her in front of my apartment house."

"I can't imagine abandoning a pet, especially a baby." She glanced at her daughter, and Katie understood she didn't want to say more about it in front of her child. "I'm glad she found a good home."

"I take her to the Senior Home to visit. The residents there love her."

Haleigh approached. "May I help you with something?" she asked the woman. After a few minutes, the woman bought the spider plant.

"Bye, Chloe." The little girl waved as she walked out with her mother.

"I just wanted to make sure you were okay, Haleigh."

"Thanks. God answered our prayers for sure." Haleigh took the kitten from Katie and cuddled her under her chin. "I'm always glad for a visit from you and Chloe."

Since no customers remained in the shop, Tia Moreno, a part-time employee, came out from behind the counter to pet

Chloe. "So, your sister-in-law is all right now? Are you going to see the baby?"

"Willie and I plan to go on Saturday."

"Good." She pushed her short dark hair behind her ears. "You know my friend, Cheryl Nelson? She's ..." Tia shook her head and returned to her place at the cash register.

Katie and Haleigh looked at each other, then back at Tia. Tia examined her nails, signaling her intention to say no more. Katie surmised what Tia didn't say.

"How is Cheryl? I haven't seen her for a while," Haleigh gave Chloe back to Katie.

"She's okay, I guess." Tia shrugged.

A couple entered the shop and cut off their conversation.

As Haleigh moved to wait on the customers, Katie decided to leave. "Bye, Tia. See you later, Haleigh." With Chloe in her arms, she exited the shop.

JACKSON WANTED to find a way to connect with Katie Mann other than at the Senior Home when he visited his grandfather, so he drove to Greenlawn right after school and pulled up in front of Floral Creations.

He tapped on his steering wheel. He didn't have her phone number or her address, but he knew her friend Haleigh Abbott worked at Floral Creations. Haleigh probably wouldn't give him Katie's personal information, but he could order some flowers for her and put a personal message on the card. Then someone from the florist shop could deliver them to her home.

He could have them delivered to the Senior Home, but that might make too public a statement and cause her to put up her wall again.

Getting out of his car, he took a deep breath and opened the shop door to the jingle of a bell.

He breathed in the scent of flowers and earth and looked

around. Potted houseplants, mums, and autumn arrangements filled the shop. A young woman with short dark hair helped a customer at the cash register. Katie's friend talked to a customer in the greenhouse. A young man with short dark auburn hair rose from a desk in what looked to be the office and came toward him with a smile. Probably Will White, the florist.

"May I help you?"

"Yes, at least I think so." Jackson wasn't sure how to explain his need.

Just then, Haleigh, followed by the customer, came out of the greenhouse carrying a rust-colored mum and set it on the counter by the cash register. "Tia will help you, Mrs. Hamilton."

"Thank you, Haleigh." Mrs. Hamilton smiled.

Tia ran the scanner over the label. "It's a lovely plant, Mrs. Hamilton. Are you buying it as a gift?"

Haleigh wiped her hands on her jeans and turned toward Jackson and Will. "Jackson, what a nice surprise to see you here."

It might be easier to talk about his mission with Haleigh. "Hi, Haleigh."

The other man's eyebrows lifted in surprise. Haleigh laid her hand on his arm.

"Jackson Stone, this is my fiancé and owner of Floral Creations, Will White."

Will's warm handshake and friendly manner made Jackson feel at ease.

"Good to meet you, Jackson."

"Same here."

"I met Jackson the other day when I went to the Senior Home with Katie and Chloe. Jackson's grandfather, David Stone, is a resident and a friend of Mary Davis," Haleigh said to Will.

Will nodded. "I often deliver to the Home, but I've never met your grandfather."

Jackson chuckled and shook his head. "No, I guess we don't often think of giving my grandfather flowers, although my grandmother had beautiful flower beds."

Will grinned. "I have some work to do in my office, so I'll leave you in Haleigh's capable hands." Will shared a look of mutual tenderness with Haleigh. Jackson would have known they were in love, even if he didn't know they were engaged.

Haleigh turned to him as Will walked away. "So, how may I help you, Jackson?"

He lowered his voice and turned so the young woman at the counter couldn't hear what he said. "I want to get some flowers ... for Katie. And I hope you'll deliver them for me."

"That shouldn't be a problem."

"The thing is," Jackson tucked his hands in his pockets, "I don't want them delivered to her workplace, and I don't know where she lives."

The petite brunette nodded. "I do." She bit her lip and folded her hands in front of her. "I don't want you to take this the wrong way, Jackson, but Katie is my best friend next to Willie. I can't give you her address or her telephone number."

"I know. But you can still make sure she gets the flowers?"

"Yes."

He decided it would be all right to confide in Haleigh. "I want to get to know her better. I promise you I'm not out to hurt her or take advantage. This is the only way I can figure out to get her attention, other than at the Home, and there we have an audience. You know who I mean?" He didn't like to think of his grandfather as a troublemaker, but Grandpa and Mary often made comments that embarrassed him and Katie.

"Yes, I do. They mean well, and at least they're on your side." She signaled Jackson to follow her to a display of cut flowers. "Katie's favorite color is pink, and her favorite flowers are lilies."

An arrangement of pink lilies caught his eye. "Consider the lilies of the field, how they grow ... yet Solomon in all his glory was not arrayed like one of these."

"Matthew six." Haleigh faced him. "Are you a Christian, Jackson?"

"I am. At ten, I walked the aisle at church and received the Lord Jesus Christ as my Savior."

"Katie attends Greenlawn Bible Church, if you're ever in town on Sunday. Maybe you'd like to come to our Christmas play. Katie's in charge of drama productions at our church."

"Thanks for the invitation. I'll keep that in mind."

"So, let's see about the flowers."

A little later Jackson got back in his car and drove to the Senior Home to visit his grandfather, satisfied that the bouquet of pink lilies with his personal message attached would make its way to the dwelling place of one lovely redhead with sparkling green eyes.

KATIE, dressed for work, opened the door to find a bouquet of beautiful pink lilies thrust toward her. She sucked in her breath. "W-what?"

Haleigh's grinning face appeared. "I am delivering an order for one Katie Mann. Does she live here?"

Katie glanced at Haleigh, then back at the flowers. "Y-yes, but ..." She took a breath and frowned. "I hope they're not from Nathan. If so, take them back."

Haleigh shifted the vase of flowers to one side and shook her head, her eyes sparkling. "No, not Nathan. A secret admirer ordered these for you." She handed the vase to Katie. Katie stepped back and allowed her to enter the apartment. Haleigh closed the door.

"They're beautiful, but who?" Katie walked to the kitchen and set the vase on the table.

"Read the card and find out."

Katie took the card and read it several times. Warmth spread throughout her body. She looked at her friend, wide-eyed. "Jackson Stone? He sent me flowers. Pink lilies!" Katie pulled out a chair and sat down, breathless, pleased, incredulous, and uncertain. "He-he wants to go out with me!"

Haleigh placed her hand over Katie's. "Why are you so surprised? Jackson really likes you, and he wants to get to know you other than at the Senior Home under prying eyes." Haleigh raised her eyebrows, and Katie nodded.

"I can't tell you what to do, girlfriend, but I do like Jackson. I think he's a man you can trust. It's sweet that he came to the shop to order flowers for you, but he didn't try to find out your address or telephone number. He said sending them to the Senior Home would be too public. I promised him you'd get them. Willie likes him, too, and Willie's a pretty good judge of character."

Katie caressed a soft petal with her fingertips and looked once again at the card in her hand. "He wrote his cell number on the card." Katie compared Jackson and Nathan in her mind. She wanted to trust Jackson, tell him the truth about her past, and believe he'd still want a relationship with her.

Haleigh reached out to give Katie a hug. "Well, I'd better go. Willie and I have an appointment tonight with Pastor Pete to start our pre-marriage counseling, and I know you have to go to work." She walked toward the door, then turned back. "Oh, by the way, I invited Jackson to church. He said he's been a Christian since he was ten."

Katie, still in a daze, remained seated and stared at the flowers as Haleigh let herself out. The scent of the lilies permeated the air. She chuckled. Her shy friend knew a lot about Jackson. How did Haleigh know so much?

She shook her head to clear it. Katie didn't want to be late for work. She set the card next to the vase and read it repeatedly as she prepared and ate her supper.

9

Jackson unlocked his apartment door and set his bulging backpack on the table, tired from the school day and the teachers' meeting afterward. He pulled his phone out of his pocket and checked it for the umpteenth time. Still no response from Katie.

Disappointed, he laid the phone on the table. Did the twenty-four-hour wait mean her answer was no?

She'd probably worked all night and hadn't had time to call. But she could have texted.

If he had her phone number, he'd call her. At the time, sending the date invitation with the flowers seemed like the right choice, but maybe she'd prefer to be asked in person.

He lowered himself into his stuffed recliner, one of the few comforts in his sparsely furnished apartment. He fingered the TV remote, then picked up a copy of the college yearbook lying on the floor beside his chair. Without effort, the book opened to the page that held Katie Mann's senior portrait.

Her red curls framed her oval face with its clear complexion, and her rosy lips and green eyes smiled at him. What would it be like to see that smile every day for the rest of his life, to come home to her instead of an empty apartment? She'd already won his heart. If only he could win her confidence. One day, when the time was right, he'd ask Katie to marry him.

He must have dozed off because he suddenly started at a tweet from his phone. A text message. He blinked a couple of times, then jumped up to retrieve his phone from the table. A text from Katie. Holding his breath, he opened the message. He leaped and shouted. "Whoopie! She said yes!"

"Sorry," he apologized to the people downstairs, although they couldn't hear his apology. He spun around a couple of times and pumped his fist. Saving her number to his contacts, he paced through his apartment a couple of times. He really wanted to call her right now, but she had to work tonight. He texted her, letting her know he'd received her message and that he'd call her tomorrow afternoon.

He set about fixing his supper, humming and whistling as he worked.

"A HAYRIDE? And a campfire with hot dogs and s'mores? Sounds great to me as long as I can go with you." Although Jackson had pictured a more intimate setting of a dinner date with Katie, the church activity sounded like fun.

"Are you sure, Jackson? The hayride and campfire event is an annual tradition for the young adults at Greenlawn Bible Church, and it's lots of fun. But if you'd rather not ..."

He leaned back in his chair and switched the phone to his other ear. "No, no. It sounds great. It's been a long time since I went on a hayride and got to stuff hay down someone's neck." He grinned as he waited for her response.

A few seconds passed before Katie said, "I'll be sure to wear a tight collar Friday night."

Jackson chuckled. "What time should I pick you up?" He held his breath, unsure whether she would trust him with her address.

"We'll meet in the church parking lot at six, then carpool out to the farm. You can pick me up at five forty-five."

He let out his breath. "Um, how do I get to your house?"

"Oh, that's right. You do have to know where I live." She gave him the address and directions to get there. "When we get to church, we'll ride with Haleigh and Willie. Willie will put the seats back in his van so eight of us can fit in." It took a few seconds for all the information to sink into his brain. "Jackson, is it really okay with you?"

He heard the uncertainty in her voice and hurried to reassure her. "Really, Katie, we'll have a good time. I attend church on Sundays, but I haven't been involved in other activities lately. I like hayrides and campfires, and I'm looking forward to spending time with you."

"Thank you." She spoke softly. "I'm looking forward to it too."

Jackson wanted more time, more things to say to keep her on the phone, but they ended their conversation. He sensed Katie's relief that he'd agreed to attend the group event with her, remembering that she'd preferred group events during college. He shrugged. A group date or with her alone, it didn't matter to him so long as he could spend time with her. Hopefully, it would be their first date of many.

He wasn't sure how he'd survive until Friday night.

"OH, NO!" Katie muttered the words softly when she saw Nathan West standing beside Derek Hall in the church parking lot.

Jackson touched her arm. "Is everything okay?"

She smiled up at Jackson. "Yes." She tried to keep a casual tone and hoped Jackson wouldn't ask any more questions. And she prayed Nathan would stay away.

Katie wore blue jeans and a bright pink turtleneck sweater.

She also wore a warm black jacket with a pink knit hat, gloves, and scarf, and sturdy hiking boots with warm socks. Katie knew the campfire later would be most welcome on a cold evening like this.

With Haleigh and Willie, she and Jackson made a foursome. "We've got your back," Haleigh whispered to her as they prepared to get into Willie's van. "Derek invited Nathan tonight."

"Thanks," Katie whispered back, especially relieved when Derek and Nathan got into the church van. She felt Jackson's hand on her elbow, and a shiver passed through her. He helped her into Willie's van and sat beside her in the second seat. A young man sat down next to Jackson, someone Katie didn't know.

"Paul Miliken," he said, offering his hand to Jackson.

Jackson shook it. "Jackson Stone. Good to meet you. And this is Katie Mann."

Katie nodded and said hello.

Caitlin, Anita, and Lori crowded into the back seat. Paul began a conversation with them.

Haleigh smiled at her from the front seat, and Katie heard the murmur of voices around her. Mostly she was aware of the man beside her. When she looked at Jackson, he was watching her.

He dipped his head toward her. "What are you thinking?" The whisper of his warm breath tickled her ear, and she caught the scent of his aftershave. "You're very quiet tonight."

Katie shifted her thoughts quickly away from Nathan, not ready to tell Jackson the one thing about her past that might make her lose him. "I'm sorry. I have a lot on my mind." She shifted her body slightly so she could see him better. "How is school?"

"Good." He straightened in the seat. "We're getting toward the end of the quarter so the kids are finishing their term projects."

"Has it been a good year? Are you happy being a teacher?"

"I love teaching as much as you love nursing, although I'm not looking forward to the graduate courses I'm going to take in January."

"Are you getting your master's degree?"

"I don't have to, but I want to."

Katie nodded. "You'll be busy with teaching and taking classes. You won't have time for much else." Her stomach sank. Jackson might not have time for her. Then she scolded herself. If God wanted them together, they would have time, and Jackson would make the time.

He picked up her gloved hand and leaned toward her again. "I'll always have time for you, Miss Kate." He squeezed her hand.

Warmth enveloped her. She squeezed his hand back.

Willie stopped his van when they arrived at the farm. Wagons loaded with bales of hay stood ready. "Everybody out!" He opened his door and jumped out.

They piled out of the vehicle and climbed on one of the waiting wagons, their breath coming out in frosty puffs. Bales of hay lined the sides, and straw lay scattered on the wooden floor of the wagon. Katie and Jackson shared a hay bale, still holding hands, with Haleigh and Willie next to them. Some of the young adults sat on the floor. Uneasy, Katie looked around but didn't see Nathan on their wagon.

Soon they were off. The noisy tractor made conversation difficult, but they managed to talk by leaning close to one another.

"Wouldn't it be fun to have Aubrey and Jeremy here tonight?" Haleigh asked Katie.

Jackson put a finger beside his mouth. "Let's see. Jeremy is Haleigh's brother and Aubrey is ...?"

Willie pointed to his chest with a gloved hand. "My sister."

"And now you two are getting married. Keeping it all in the

family. Less problem for you to know how to split up the holidays."

"How are they doing?" Katie asked. "I haven't heard from Aubrey lately."

"Well, you know they've been pretty busy. Jeremy has a heavy course load and an internship this semester, and Aubrey is teaching. But Jeremy says he wouldn't have it any other way. Being married to Aubrey this year is so much better than living across campus from her."

Willie pulled a piece of hay from the bale they sat on and tickled Haleigh's nose with it. "Remember how much fun we had, picking on you girls, stuffing hay down your necks?"

Haleigh grabbed the hay away from Willie and rubbed her nose. "Willie, behave."

He grinned. "But I am." He put his arm around her and pulled her close.

Katie looked at Jackson, who winked at her. "I'm protected. I wore a high collar tonight. And a scarf."

Jackson raised his eyebrows and cocked his head. "You know the saying, 'where there's a will, there's a way.'"

Several of the young adults began to discuss the group's Christmas party, and they were all drawn into the discussion. Katie and Jackson joined in when they started singing favorite praise songs, hymns, and even some Christmas carols.

As she became more comfortable with Jackson beside her, Katie forgot to watch out for Nathan. She dropped the wall of protection she had kept in place for so long. Surely, she could trust Jackson.

Maybe Jackson was the man God had for her. She put the brakes on her runaway thoughts. Although she had known Jackson for several years, this was, after all, their first date. The first, with many more to come, she hoped.

It didn't take long for Jackson to become a part of the group, and for everyone to recognize Greenlawn's Katie Mann and her friend Jackson Stone as a couple.

Anita, Caitlin, and Lori managed to pull her aside during the campfire.

"Where did you find Jackson, Katie?" Caitlin giggled.

"I didn't know you had a boyfriend." Anita sounded insulted.

Katie's recent acquaintance with Jackson had been confined to the Senior Home, and this was the first time most of the young adults from church had met him. Katie had never mentioned him during play practice.

"He's certainly a well-kept secret," Lori said.

Should she respond to their curiosity or evade their questions? It was best to be up front with the young women. Katie didn't like gossip, and she wasn't ashamed of being seen with Jackson.

"No secret. Jackson and I first met at college. His grandfather lives at the Senior Home, and I saw Jackson again one day when he was visiting his grandfather."

"Does he have brothers?" Lori asked. The three young women giggled.

Katie smiled and shrugged. "A younger one, I think. They don't live around here."

A few paces away, Jackson talked with Paul and Willie. From the other side of the bonfire, Nathan watched her. *Oh, no!* He waved and started toward her.

Quickly, she excused herself and hurried back to Jackson's side. She glanced over her shoulder but didn't see Nathan. Haleigh moved in beside her on the other side.

"Is everything all right?" Haleigh whispered.

"The girls were curious about Jackson, and Nathan spotted me. I wish he'd stay away." Katie didn't want anything to spoil what she had going with Jackson.

Haleigh squeezed her friend's arm. "I doubt that he'll try anything with so many people around."

Katie shook her head. "I'm not so sure. He thinks because he's a Christian now, we should get back together." She knew now she'd made a serious mistake going to the play with him.

AFTER THEY SAID goodnight to Haleigh and Willie and got out of Willie's van in the church parking lot, Jackson walked Katie to his dark blue SUV. He'd just opened the door for her when Nathan walked up behind her.

"You didn't introduce me to your friend, Katie."

Katie whirled around as Jackson turned to see who spoke.

The heat rose up Katie's neck and into her face. Her stomach clenched. What she feared most was happening, leaving her momentarily speechless. Jackson rescued her.

He held out his hand to Nathan. "I'm Jackson Stone."

Nathan shook his hand. "Nathan West. An old friend of Katie's." He glanced from Jackson to Katie. "Have you known each other long?"

Not that it was any of his business. "Nathan, please ..."

"We met in college. We had some classes together. And we met again recently." Jackson clasped her hand.

Katie was grateful for his intervention in this awkward situation. If she spoke to Nathan right now, she might not be gracious.

She turned to Jackson. "Jackson, I'd like to go home."

"Nice to make your acquaintance." Jackson nodded at Nathan and moved aside so Katie could slide into the seat. He stood protectively by the car door, preventing Nathan from approaching closer.

"Katie and I are old friends."

Please Nathan, don't!

"We went to school together. Have her tell you about it sometime."

Derek came up to them and held out his hand to Jackson. "Derek Hall. I saw you on the hayride with Katie, but I didn't get the chance to speak with you."

"Jackson Stone."

"I've been looking all over for you, Nate." Derek glanced at

Katie through the window and then back at Nathan. "What are you doing, dude? What are you up to? Leave her alone."

Derek had changed dramatically in the past four months since he became a Christian. He wouldn't give Katie's secret away because he probably didn't know it. But Nathan knew, and she was sure he would.

Derek propelled Nathan away with a hand on his shoulder.

Jackson closed Katie's door and walked around the SUV. He got in. "Are you okay? He upset you."

Katie nodded, afraid to look at Jackson. She folded her arms across her body and scrunched down in the seat. The sense of failure and shame that she thought she had put behind her resurfaced. She intended to tell him, but not now, not yet. She wanted to choose the time and place.

"CARE TO TALK ABOUT IT?" How could he help her if she wouldn't talk to him?

Katie shook her head.

Jackson started the vehicle and adjusted the heat control. He waited while the frost cleared off the windshield, hoping she would talk to him before he put it in gear and drove out into the street.

He'd enjoyed the hayride and campfire, and he thought Katie had as well. The more time he spent with her, the more he hoped for a permanent relationship with her. She'd relaxed as she interacted with her friends, people she trusted and who knew her well. They'd talked and laughed. More than once he'd caught her watching him, and she didn't look away. Her hand rested in his whenever they were side by side, and that was most of the evening.

Then Nathan West appeared and sent Katie back into her protective cocoon.

The ride to her apartment was short and quiet. He parked

the SUV and turned off the engine. As cold as it was, he didn't want to keep her out much longer.

As they walked up to her door, she didn't shrug his arm away from her shoulders, but she didn't say a word. Gently he turned her toward him, and with his finger under her chin, lifted her face toward him. Tears stood in her eyes, and she rolled her lips and pressed them together.

"Katie, please tell me what's wrong."

"You might never want to see me again," she choked out.

He wiped away two tears that slid down her cheeks. "That's not true, Katie Mann. I'm sure there's nothing you've done that's unforgiveable or would make me not want to see you again."

She shook her head. He dropped his hand, and she lowered her gaze.

When she shivered, he knew he had to let her go in.

He lifted her hand and kissed it. "Remember, Katie, I'll keep coming back. I believe God intends for the two of us to be together. I can wait until you're ready to tell me. I'll be here." He let go of her hand. "You'd better go in now."

She fumbled for her key, which he took from her hand and unlocked the door. "Good night." He handed the key back to her.

"Good night," she whispered. She rushed inside and up the stairs.

Jackson slowly turned and walked to his SUV. He watched until her apartment light went on before getting into his vehicle and starting the engine. Then he leaned his forehead against the steering wheel.

"I don't know what happened, God. We had a great time together until Nathan came along. Please help Katie. Help me. I think I love her, and I believe You want us together. Take away her hurt. Help her to trust You and to trust me enough to tell me what's bothering her. I'm not sure what Nathan West was trying to do or say, but Katie's hurting."

He drove back to his apartment with plenty of time to think. Tomorrow, he had to spend the morning reading student essays.

Lunchtime and the afternoon were committed to a get-together with his mother's side of the family, and who knew how long into the evening that would last. He shook his head. Not a good day.

Perhaps Sunday, he could take her out to dinner. Maybe she would talk then, and they could get things straightened out. He hoped so.

CURLED UP IN BED, Katie stared into the darkness, sleep eluding her. Angry with Nathan and feeling foolish for leaving Jackson as she did, she found it difficult to pray.

If God had forgiven her, why did she feel such shame and guilt? Her pride. Her intimate act with Nathan had led to a teen pregnancy, and it had been a splotch on her Christian testimony. Telling Jackson would make her different in his eyes.

"God, forgive me for being too proud to trust You. Jackson's a good man. If You want us together, my past won't matter because I've repented, and You've forgiven me. Please help me to be honest with Jackson.

"And, God, forgive my anger with Nathan and stop him from pursuing me. I can't convince him that I'm not interested in a relationship with him, but You can."

Would she ever see Jackson again?

10

*J*ackson sipped his coffee. Would a text message or a phone call be the best way to contact Katie? He'd spent a restless night and had to know she was all right.

His open Bible lay before him, and he prayed for wisdom to do the right thing. He'd call her because he could tell more by the sound of her voice—if she decided to answer his call. He waited until the clock said eight.

After several rings, he thought he'd have to leave a voicemail, and he began planning what he would say.

"Hello."

He let out his breath. "Katie, hi. It's Jackson."

"I know."

When she didn't continue, he licked his lips and said, "Are you okay?"

She yawned. "I'm okay. Just a little tired."

"I'm sorry. Did I wake you up?"

"It's okay. It's time for me to get up anyway."

"I waited until eight to call you."

"I'm glad you called." He loved the soft intimacy of her voice. "I had a good time last night."

He smiled. "Me too." He ran a finger over the rim of his coffee cup. "Um, Katie, I was wondering if you will go out to dinner with me tomorrow afternoon."

"Tomorrow? I have church, and then I work the night shift."

"Well, today my schedule is full. Otherwise, I'd be there this morning. This afternoon is committed to a family thing. I thought maybe I could come to your church tomorrow. And if we go out right after, you'll have plenty of time to get ready for work."

"I'd like that, Jackson." Her voice seemed to take on a smile. "Morning worship is at ten-thirty. I probably won't make it to Sunday school because I'm working tonight, but that's an hour earlier if you want to come."

"Tell you what, I'll meet you for morning worship. Whoever gets there first can save a seat for the other."

"Sounds like a plan to me." Katie yawned and giggled.

Jackson smiled. "I think you need a cup of coffee to wake you up." He carried his coffee mug to the sink and leaned against the counter. "Katie, I hope you understand that I intend to stick around no matter what." He couldn't imagine his sweet, beautiful Katie doing anything that would make him leave.

"I hope so, Jackson. But ... well, we'll talk tomorrow."

"Okay, I look forward to seeing you ... and talking."

"Me too."

"I hope you don't mind if I call you again later."

"No, I don't mind."

"Bye, Miss Kate."

"Bye, Jackson."

KATIE COULD NO LONGER HOLD off telling Jackson about her relationship with Nathan West and about the baby. He deserved to learn the truth from her—not someone else—and especially not from Nathan. By tomorrow she'd know whether

Jackson would keep his promise to stick around no matter what.

Her phone rang again as she fixed her breakfast. Haleigh.

"Wasn't last night fun?" Haleigh's cheerful voice lifted her spirits. "I'm glad Jackson came with you. Willie and I both like him."

Katie nodded, although her friend couldn't see her. "I had a good time with Jackson. He is special ... wonderful!" She pushed her hair behind her ear.

"I'm glad Nathan didn't pester you. I guess having Jackson with you made him see he didn't have a chance with you."

"Well, about that." Katie leaned against the kitchen counter. Her spirits sank. "As we were getting into Jackson's SUV, Nathan came over and introduced himself. Then he said ..." she choked out the words. "He said I should tell Jackson about our time in school together. I wanted to crawl some place and hide."

"Aw, Katie, did he really? The nerve of him. I'm so sorry."

"I am too. I'm going to tell Jackson, but I want it to be in my own time, not when Nathan tries to embarrass me into it." Katie tapped the countertop with her fingers.

"How did Jackson take it? What did he say?"

She wrapped her free arm around her middle. "Oh, Haleigh, Jackson was wonderful! He was so gracious to Nathan—better than I'd have been if I'd been able to talk. And he was so considerate of me."

Haleigh sighed. "Have you decided what you're going to do now?"

"Jackson is taking me out to dinner after church tomorrow. In fact, he's coming to Greenlawn Bible for morning worship. Will you and Willie pray for me? I'm going to tell him about my relationship with Nathan and about the baby. I have to. I can't go on hiding the truth. I'm so afraid Nathan or someone else might tell him."

"Of course, we'll pray. I'm convinced you and Jackson belong together."

"I hope so. We'll see. I'm going to spend some time with Chloe this morning, then come back here and sleep again. I have to work tonight."

"It's time for me to leave for work. Willie and I are going to my parents' house overnight to celebrate my birthday, so we won't be in church tomorrow morning to see Jackson."

"Oh, that's right. See you when you get back. And happy birthday!"

A few minutes later, Katie headed out. Although uncertain she could face her parents without crying, she prepared to tell them about Jackson.

Today, she had a brief reprieve. Neither of them was home when she arrived. They probably already knew about Jackson anyway. They lived in a small town, after all, and people talked. Maybe they would wait for her to tell them when she was ready.

Playing with Chloe made her laugh, and the cuddly, purring kitten lifted her spirits, although a mental picture of Jackson holding Chloe clenched at her heart.

After tomorrow, would Jackson withdraw his vow to never go away?

On her next day off, she had to take Chloe to visit at the Senior Home. It had been a week since their last visit, and the residents looked forward to seeing the kitten. Right now, sleep was hailing her. She gave Chloe one last cuddle, made sure the door was locked, and headed back to her apartment.

SHIFTING INTO WORK MODE, Katie pushed her trouble to the back of her mind so she could give the residents proper care. Several residents' family members shared their concerns about their loved ones. The many visitors that day and an evening Thanksgiving program put on by a local 4-H club left the residents stimulated and restless, so it took a while to settle them down.

Mally, the nurse's aide, came to her during her break time with tears in her eyes.

"Katie, I'm so sorry."

"What's the problem?"

"It's Everett again. He had to get up to use the bathroom and won't go back to bed. He keeps telling me to leave him alone, he has his rights. I think he has something against me. Anyway, I told him he should start acting like an adult, not a child, and I came to get you before I said or did something I'd be sorry for."

Everett was a sweet man during the day, but at night he sometimes became uncooperative.

"Okay, why don't you take a few moments to cool down, and I'll check on Everett."

"Thanks, Katie."

After getting Everett calmed and back in bed, she checked on the residents in their rooms. By midnight, they were all in bed. Quiet reigned, and Katie took a lunch break.

Home after her shift and wanting only sleep, she showered and fell into bed for a brief nap. When her alarm awakened her, she rushed to get ready for church on time and prepare for dinner with Jackson afterward.

The green dress she wore accented her eyes, and she left her hair down, curls framing her face. She parked her car at church just as Jackson pulled into the parking lot.

As she waited for him by the church steps, her heart raced. He approached, his eyes focused on her and a smile on his face. Her insides trembled, and she wished with all her heart that their talk was behind them, to hear Jackson say once again, "I intend to stay," and mean it.

He grasped her hand. "Good morning, Miss Kate." His greeting soothed her.

"It's good to see you." She wanted to hug him and thank him for being there. She wanted to memorize that smile and the way he looked at her. Because it could be the last time.

Together they walked in and found a seat about midway

back. Several people turned in their seats and greeted them. Some young adults who'd been on the hayride stopped to speak to them.

Katie looked around. She didn't see Nathan, although Derek sat beside his mother a few rows ahead of them. Nathan had told her he was active in his own church. She checked for Cheryl and Lars. Her heart ached for the absent young couple, and she prayed silently for them.

Jackson leaned toward her and said quietly, "You look tired, Katie. Did you have a busy night?"

With her hand over her mouth, she tried to stifle a yawn. "Yes, a busy, busy night. It took a long time to get everyone quieted down, and there were more problems than usual. But I made it."

"You're here and looking lovely. Green is your color. And I like your hair down."

Katie blushed at the compliments. She appreciated that Jackson noticed the color of her dress. The admiration in his eyes made it hard to breath. "Thank you. Pink is my favorite color, but I like green almost as well." She pulled on a curl. "I'm glad you came today."

"Me too." He glanced around. "I don't see Haleigh and Willie."

Katie shook her head. "No, they went to Wellsburg after work yesterday to celebrate Haleigh's birthday with her family."

"Sorry to miss them. But there'll be other times."

"I hope so." When his gaze connected with hers, she lowered her eyes first.

The music for the opening hymn began, and they stood with the rest of the congregation.

The now familiar scent of his aftershave and the warmth of his body beside her kept her acutely aware of Jackson and made it difficult for Katie to concentrate on worship. Pastor Pete's text for the day was Romans 8:28: "*And we know that all things work together for good to them that love God, to those who are called according to His purpose."*

"Bad things do happen to God's people," Pastor Pete said. "He doesn't promise a painless, problem-free life, but He does promise His goodness when we seek His will, when we obey and follow Him. God is good, and He wants what's best for His children. This promise can bring comfort to a troubled heart."

Telling Jackson about her past indiscretion was the right thing to do.

Father God, You love me and want the best for me. If You want us together, we'll get through this afternoon. And if not ... well, help me to accept Your will. Life without Jackson looked bleak.

Since that September day when she'd met him in the common room at work, she'd fallen in love with him. His smile, his kindness and love for his grandfather, his sensitivity toward her, as well as his tenderness with Chloe, drew her to him.

She glanced at him as he listened to the sermon. He caught her gaze and smiled, and butterflies danced in her stomach.

His was not the surface charm of a man like Nathan, but something deeper, which he drew from a source other than himself. She could trust him.

Katie wanted her parents to meet Jackson, for them to know she could make a good choice in men. But would she have that opportunity once she told him the truth?

Her eyes closed. The warmth of his hand as he entwined his fingers with hers sent a current up her arm. Her eyes popped open.

He leaned toward her and whispered, "You were falling asleep."

Her face hot, she glanced around to see if anyone else noticed. Fully awake now, she took a deep breath and let it out slowly.

She didn't remember singing the final hymn or hearing the benediction. She must have sounded normal to her friends, because none of them looked at her as though she'd sprouted horns.

Jackson stood and let her out into the aisle ahead of him.

"I hoped to meet your parents this morning. Do they attend church here?"

"My mother got called to work, and my dad is away on business. Otherwise, they'd be here."

To introduce Jackson to her parents today would have been awkward, and they didn't have time to stay and visit. The need to tell Jackson the truth became more urgent, and Katie had to get some sleep soon.

11

In the quickly filling Hillside Diner, the hostess led Katie and Jackson to a corner booth that allowed them some privacy.

They ordered, and as they waited for their food, Jackson told her about his family party the day before.

"I really want my family to meet you, Katie. Do you think you can come home with me sometime between Christmas and New Year's, if not sooner?"

"I'd like that. We'll see." If he still wanted her to go after today.

"You said you agreed to take a day shift for a coworker so she could have the day with her family on Thanksgiving. Will you be able to celebrate at all with your family?"

"Well, Mom will save some food for me, and after work I'll go to my parents' house to visit with the relatives who are still there."

Jackson chuckled. "What do you think Chloe will do with the crowd of people?"

Katie waved her fork. "I think she might be a little afraid at first, but no one is a stranger to Chloe for long. She won't be lacking someone to hold her for most of the day."

Katie pushed back her empty plate, and Jackson did the same. She couldn't put him off any longer.

"Jackson, I have something to tell you." He knew that already. She forced herself to meet his eyes before lowering hers to her hands folded on the table.

He nodded and leaned forward. "I'm listening." He held out his hands, inviting her to put her hands in his. She did.

This time she took a deep breath. "I want you to hear this from me. I knew I'd have to tell you, but it's hard talking about it. I don't want you to hear it from someone else ... especially not Nathan West."

He waited without speaking.

"You probably wondered why I didn't date during college." He nodded, and she continued, "I liked you then, Jackson. But I was afraid to ... to trust myself alone with a guy."

He wrinkled his forehead, and she could see the question in his eyes, although he didn't say anything. Instead, he squeezed her hand, encouraging her to continue.

They broke handholds and leaned back when the waitress approached to ask them if they wanted dessert. Katie shook her head when Jackson looked at her. "No, thank you," he told the waitress. She laid the check on the table next to Jackson and collected their dishes.

He leaned forward again and clasped her hands. "Go on."

She had his full attention. She couldn't let this moment pass.

"Nathan and I were in school together. We both joined drama club during middle school, and we became very good friends." She paused and licked her lips. He watched her but didn't speak. "I was a latchkey kid. My parents worked more and more, and they became so involved in their professional lives, it was like we weren't a family anymore. In fact, my mom and dad almost got divorced."

Her voice trembled, and she paused a moment to gain control. Jackson's eyes remained fixed on her face. She lowered her eyes and stared at their hands.

"Haleigh Abbott and Aubrey White were my best friends. We were known as the Three Sisters. We did everything together. And since I didn't have any brothers of my own, their brothers became like brothers to me. I spent a lot of time with them when my parents weren't home. But when I got to know Nathan and joined the drama club, all that changed. Nathan became the center of my life. My dad wasn't around much, and I spent more and more time with Nathan."

Jackson nodded, and she wondered what he was thinking. She swallowed hard.

"One day, when we were in high school, I decided to take him to my house when my parents weren't there, something they'd forbidden. I knew the rules. I knew it was wrong. I was going against all I had been taught as a Christian. Nathan was kind and charming, and he finally convinced me it was okay, and we ... we became intimate."

Jackson's intake of breath made her look up. She saw the shock on his face, but he didn't release her hands. In fact, he tightened his grasp.

She forced herself to look into his eyes. "Only once. But at sixteen, I became pregnant."

Studying his face, she couldn't decipher what he was thinking, but she rushed on.

"My dad wanted me to have an abortion, but I knew that was wrong. I carried a baby, a human life within me. My grandmother took me in, homeschooled me, and when I had the baby, I gave him up for adoption. By then, Nathan had disappeared." Tears came to her eyes. "I hurt so much, but it was the best choice for the baby. Nathan and I weren't ready to be parents. The baby has a mother and father to care for him now."

Although she wanted to wipe at the tears running down her cheeks, she didn't want to let go of Jackson's hands.

She waited. Jackson didn't let go, and he didn't get up and leave.

"So that's why you always put up a wall when a guy tries to

get close?" Jackson's voice was a hoarse whisper.

"I know that God has forgiven me for my sin, but I can't entirely let go of the shame of failure. I failed God, I failed my parents, and I failed my friends. And I don't want to lose you, Jackson."

His jaw worked, and he turned his face away from her. Was he angry with her? He let go of her hands and sat back. She grabbed a napkin to wipe her eyes and nose. Was he going to get up and walk out? She laid her hands over her stomach.

"I'm ... I'm falling in love with you, and I don't want to lose you. I've been so afraid someone else would tell you. And when Nathan said what he did Friday night ..."

He shook his head. "I'm sorry that happened to you, Katie. You both were young and did something you regretted. Nathan took advantage of you, and he's still trying to take advantage of you." He leaned toward her. "I meant what I said. I'm here to stay."

"Are you sure? I'm not the pure girl you thought I was."

He reached out to her, and she placed her hands in his. "Purity is a matter of the heart. There are things in my past that I'm not proud of. We all make wrong choices. The Bible says we all sin and need forgiveness."

She swallowed, trying to ease the lump in her throat. "I want you to be sure." She added quickly before he could say more, "During this next week, we will not see each other or call one another. I want you to pray and search your heart to make certain you're sure."

He grasped her hands tighter. "Katie—"

"If our relationship becomes permanent ..." She licked her lips, hoping she didn't assume too much. "If our relationship becomes permanent, I don't ever want to see regret in your eyes or think you're sorry you stayed with me."

He held her gaze briefly. "All right, my sweet Miss Kate. We'll do it your way." He sighed. "A week ... is a long time."

"I know." *An eternity*. She almost said never mind.

"I'll be allowed to see you next Sunday?"

She nodded. "Next Sunday."

"If I meet you in church next Sunday, you'll know I'm sure."

She nodded.

He paid for their meals and drove her back to her car in the church parking lot.

"You know you're asking a hard thing, don't you, Katie?"

"I know."

JACKSON MISSED KATIE ALREADY, although they'd just said goodbye. The week stretched endlessly before him. He felt sure now that he wanted to spend the rest of his life with her, but he would respect her wishes to wait a week.

She'd opened her heart to him in her confession, purposely making herself vulnerable to his rejection. Sweet, vibrant Katie had done the unexpected.

He wanted to punch Nathan for hurting her. He certainly didn't get a good first or second impression of Katie's so-called friend. Then he remembered they'd been young and enticed by temptation.

Proverbs 28:13 came to mind, a verse he'd learned in Sunday school as a boy, *"He who covers his sins will not prosper, but whoever confesses and forsakes them will have mercy."* He believed Katie had received God's forgiveness when she confessed her sin to God. Now Nathan couldn't hold the past over her head because she'd told Jackson.

He needed time to pray about his attitude. The past was the past. He had to be sure that he'd never allow Katie's past to stand between them, and he had to convince her he wouldn't.

After leaving Katie at her apartment, he headed for the Senior Home to visit his grandfather. Grandpa sat alone in his room, reading a book. Jackson knocked on the partially opened door.

"Come in." Grandpa greeted him with a huge smile. "Jackson, I was hoping you'd stop by today!"

"Hi, Grandpa. How are you doing?" He leaned over to embrace the older man. "Having a quiet time in your room this afternoon?" He pulled a second chair to face his grandfather and sat down.

"Yes. Well, we had a church service right after lunch, and I felt like coming in here to think over the sermon. And I have this good book to read. I'll go out to the common room later."

Jackson asked Grandpa about his book, a novel by one of Grandpa's favorite authors. "I'm just beginning the second chapter. So far, it has my attention. I'm wondering how the hero will get himself out of the pickle he's in." He closed the book. "What have you been up to?"

"I've been busy at school." Grandpa nodded. "And I went on a hayride Friday night with the young adults from Katie's church."

The old man grinned. "So, you finally took my advice, Jack, my boy!"

"I did. We had a great time. Today I attended the Greenlawn Bible Church with Katie, and we went out for dinner afterward." Jackson stopped and looked down at his shoes. He wasn't sure how much he wanted or needed to tell his grandfather.

"Is something wrong? You seem troubled."

This was between Katie and him. He shrugged and looked up. "Will you pray for me?"

"Prayer is always a good thing in any situation." His grandfather's expression held questions he wouldn't answer. He couldn't risk betraying her trust by telling him everything.

Jackson nodded. "I know. But will you pray for Katie and me this week?"

Grandpa wrinkled his brow and nodded. "Of course, Jackson." Grandpa would pray. God knew the details.

"Thank you."

To lighten the mood and change the subject, Jackson told his grandfather about the party with his mother's side of the family on Saturday. Grandpa knew the family, and he laughed heartily as Jackson talked.

"You're good for me, Jackson. Thank you for not forgetting this old man."

"How could I forget you, Grandpa? Grandma always said we were like two peas in a pod." He stood and hugged his grandfather. "I have to go now. If I don't get back here before then, I'll see you at the farm for Thanksgiving."

Grandpa got up and laid his book on top of the dresser. "I'm looking forward to seeing everyone. The hardest thing about living here is that I don't see the family as much."

"I'm sorry you couldn't stay at the farm." Jackson, away at college, hadn't been a part of the decision made for his grandfather to move to the Senior Home. He couldn't imagine what it must have been like for a man who'd lived in one place for more than fifty years to have to move out and live with strangers.

"No, my boy, I had some say in coming here. We agreed I needed more watching during the day when everyone was gone, and I have a lot of friends and activities here. It's just that as I get older ..." He sighed, then smiled. "I'll walk you out on my way to the common room. Mary should be there, and I believe there's a good movie on television this afternoon."

On his way out, Grandpa grabbed his cane from the corner by the door. He used his cane regularly now when he left his room. A sudden, sad realization hit Jackson—his grandfather was no longer the strong, hearty man he'd always known. How many more years of life did Grandpa have? Would his children have the privilege of knowing their great-grandfather?

The week ahead promised to be busy with classwork, teachers' meetings, and a couple of conferences with parents on Tuesday night. He only hoped he could do his work well while Katie intruded on his thoughts.

12

Katie had the day before Thanksgiving off from work, so she helped her mother prepare for the next day's festivities. In between tasks, she took Chloe to the Senior Home for a visit. Haleigh joined her there, along with Aubrey, who was in Greenlawn with Jeremy to celebrate the holiday with the White family. The Three Sisters enjoyed being together for the first time since summer, which made the day almost perfect for Katie.

Almost. Not seeing or talking to Jackson for a week was harder than she'd thought it would be, especially because of the uncertain outcome.

Comfortable visiting on her own, Chloe gave each resident an allotment of time, purring and mewing her way around the common room, to the delight of everyone. But the young cat kept returning to David Stone, licking his hand, sniffing his cheek, and lying on his shoulder.

Katie waited to talk about personal matters with her friends until they stepped outside the building after their visit with the residents. "So, how is everything going, Aubrey? Is Jeremy treating you well?"

"Jeremy treats me like a princess. It's like we're still on our honeymoon. He always finds time to do something special, even though he's so busy with school and church."

"Are you ever sorry you didn't wait until after he finished seminary to get married?"

"No regrets, although sometimes it's hard because we're so busy. It's easier being married than it was when we were single, living across campus from each other."

Haleigh touched her arm. "Will you have time to see Willie's house, our house, while you're in Greenlawn? Willie thinks it will be finished in time for us to move in after the wedding."

"Certainly. Can't wait." Aubrey placed her arm around her sister-in-law's shoulders and squeezed. "Your wedding plans seem to be coming along well, Haleigh." Aubrey turned toward Katie. "Haleigh said you agreed to be her maid of honor." Katie nodded. "Now, is there any romance in the air for you?"

Katie bit her lip to prevent herself from bursting into laughter. Big sister Aubrey was back.

Katie looked at Haleigh, who shrugged and shook her head slightly. Haleigh hadn't told Aubrey.

She licked her lips and knew she was blushing. "Well, there's Jackson Stone. His grandfather is David Stone, whom you met. I knew Jackson during college, and I met him here one day when he came to visit his grandfather. But we are taking some time off. I ... told him about Nathan and the baby. I want him to be sure that my past won't make a difference to him. I asked him to pray about it."

"He won't go away." Haleigh spoke with confidence the words Katie wanted to believe.

"I can't wait to meet him." Aubrey smiled and hugged Katie. "If you're supposed to be together, God will work it out," she said. "He did it for both Haleigh and me, and He'll do it for you too."

"Oh, by the way." Haleigh's voice held some excitement. "Lars Olsen came into the shop yesterday and bought a dozen red roses for Cheryl. He said he and Cheryl are getting married on Christmas Eve."

Katie's eyes widened. "Really? I haven't seen Cheryl lately. I wondered how she was doing." Katie had been praying for Cheryl and Lars and their decision about the baby. She hoped they'd spoken to Pastor Pete.

"That's nice." Aubrey bit the corner of her lip. "It's too bad Leanna won't be able to see her sister get married." Katie heard sadness in Aubrey's voice at the memory of their classmate and Aubrey's close friend.

"I'm glad they decided to get married," Haleigh said. "Willie and I have been praying for them."

"I expected they would have a big, society-type wedding. The Nelsons have a lot of money. This seems rather sudden."

Katie didn't respond verbally to Aubrey's observation. She hoped it meant that Cheryl hadn't terminated her pregnancy.

Haleigh said, "They've been engaged for a while. However, the last I knew, they hadn't set a date. Lars said their families would be together anyway, so they decided Christmas Eve would be a good time for the wedding."

Katie smiled. "I'm sure it will be a beautiful wedding. I wish them well in their marriage."

As they headed for their cars, Aubrey slipped her arm through Katie's. "Now, about this Jackson Stone."

By late Wednesday afternoon, when he drove into the parking lot at the Senior Home, Jackson ached to see Katie, and he wished for Sunday to come quickly.

Grandpa waited for him in his room, his small suitcase packed. Jackson helped him into his SUV so Grandpa could spend Thanksgiving and the weekend at the farm with his family. The weatherman promised stormless weather for the holiday weekend.

"Are you okay, Grandpa? You're rather quiet." Jackson glanced at the old man's sober face after putting the SUV into cruise.

Grandpa sighed. "I'm fine. Just thinking about Thanksgivings past and your grandmother."

"Grandma always made the best ... of everything!" Jackson gestured with one hand.

His grandfather chuckled. "I couldn't have asked for a better cook, or wife, that's for sure."

"And you're missing her a lot today."

"You can't live married to someone for almost sixty years and not miss her when she's gone. I know where she is, but there's always an empty place right here by my side and in my heart." Grandpa choked a little on the words as he placed his right hand over his heart.

Jackson blinked hard to keep the tears from clouding his eyes as he drove. Did his grandfather feel the loss so greatly that he regretted what he had with Grandma, or did the loving memories sustain him now? Would he, Jackson, ever have such a love as his grandparents with anyone ... with Katie Mann?

They talked about who would be present for the Thanksgiving celebration and who would be absent this year. The old farmhouse would ring with the voices and laughter of extended family. Jackson loved family get-togethers.

Throughout Thanksgiving Day, he often pictured Katie caring for the residents as she worked, thinking about how well she would fit into his family circle. With Grandpa already on his side, it wouldn't take long for Katie to win them all over with her bubbly personality, sparkling green eyes, and caring spirit.

His mother's voice broke into his reverie. "Is your grandfather all right, Jackson?"

"I guess so, Mom. Why do you ask?"

"I can't put my finger on it, but he doesn't seem to be himself today. Maybe he's overwhelmed by the noise and people after being in assisted living."

"Has Dad noticed anything?"

"He mentioned it a little while ago."

Jackson thought for a moment. "On the way here yesterday, he said he was thinking about Grandma and past Thanksgivings. He misses Grandma."

"Don't we all." His mother wiped her eyes. "Well, let's keep our eye on him."

Jackson nodded. He smiled when Grandpa held his sister's little girl on his lap. They seemed to be having a serious discussion. His three-year-old niece, with her blue eyes and blonde hair, had been a conversationalist since she could talk. He chuckled. Not that you could always understand her. The sweet scene of great-grandfather and great-granddaughter relieved the young man's concern for the moment.

JUST BEFORE MIDNIGHT, Jackson paced the floor of the waiting room outside the emergency department of the New Hope Hospital, waiting for his parents to arrive. He'd ridden in the ambulance with Grandpa, and now he waited while the doctor examined him.

Jackson called Katie. The sound of her voice reassured him, even though it was voicemail. "Katie, this is Jackson. I know I promised not to contact you until Sunday, but I knew you'd want to know about Grandpa Stone. We think he's had a stroke. I'm at New Hope Hospital with him now. Oh, Mom and Dad just got here. I gotta go." He ended the call and turned off his phone.

"Jackson." His father approached with his mother beside him. "Is there any news yet?" Lines of worry etched his father's face as he held tightly to Mom's hand.

This was not how or where any of them expected to spend Thanksgiving night.

"Wow, am I tired." Katie yawned and slumped back in her chair at the kitchen table.

"A busy day?" Mom set a plate filled with turkey dinner leftovers in front of her.

"Very." She unfolded her napkin. "Thanks, Mom." Inhaling the aroma of turkey made her mouth water.

"We tried to make the day special for the residents, especially the ones who had no family or friends visit them. It was so sad to see their loneliness." She laid her napkin on her lap. "We had them playing board games and doing puzzles, things like that. One of the residents played the piano, and they sang. I think they'll all settle down well tonight after all that activity. I know I will."

Dad walked in with Chloe cuddled to his chest and leaned against the counter. "I'm glad you got out of work in time to see everyone before they left."

"So am I." Most of her father's family she saw only at Thanksgiving. "I see Chloe survived the crowd."

Dad scratched the kitten's head. "When she got tired of them, she disappeared for a while. I suspect she took a nap in one of the bedrooms."

Jackson was the only one missing from her day. She longed to call him and hear his voice and share about her day, but she was the one who'd set the boundaries. Three more days. Waiting was hard.

Katie fell into bed that night, glad she had night shift the following day. Sleeping in the next morning sounded very inviting.

She awoke and checked her clock. Eight o'clock.

"Oh, well, I guess I've missed the Black Friday shopping frenzy." She chuckled at herself. She never liked shopping in crowds.

When she reached for her cell phone, it wasn't on the bedside table. She hadn't used it or seen it since before she left for work yesterday morning, and she didn't miss it because she'd been so busy. Sliding out of bed, she searched for it and found it under the sofa cushion in the living room.

"Jackson called." He must have a reason to break their agreement. She trembled as she listened to his voicemail. "Oh, no, David's in the hospital!"

When she called Jackson back, she got his voice mailbox, then settled for texting him, asking him for an update on his grandfather. She didn't have time to drive to the New Hope Hospital and back before work, and she didn't know if David had been admitted. But she activated the church prayer chain on David's behalf so her church family would be praying for him.

Just before noon, she walked to her parents' house to visit Chloe. Her father surprised her by meeting her at the kitchen door when she opened it.

He wrapped his arms around her. "Hello, Katie."

She leaned into his arms, remembering the days when her father hardly said hello to her. She kissed his cheek. "Hi, Dad. I didn't expect to see you home today."

"I didn't have anything pressing this weekend, so I gave the whole staff the time off, unless something big comes up."

"Mom had to work?"

"Today, yes, but she has tomorrow off and Sunday as well. Just Chloe and me today."

Hearing her name, the young cat walked into the kitchen. "Mew." She wound herself around Dad's legs and walked up to Katie, sniffing her. Katie stooped and lifted Chloe into her arms.

"Why don't you stay for lunch? I planned to make a sandwich with turkey leftovers. There's plenty."

Katie set the cat down and washed her hands. Father and daughter worked together to prepare their lunch from holiday leftovers. He said grace, and they began to eat. On the floor, Chloe sat like a statue, watching them closely to see if she could beg any tidbits, the tip of her tail occasionally twitching.

"So, how was the hayride last Friday?" Dad asked after swallowing his first bite.

"Fun, as usual. And we started planning the Christmas party for next month."

"And how is the drama team doing? Is the play for Christmas almost ready?"

"The team is working hard, and I expect we'll be ready on schedule."

"You seem to be enjoying it."

"Oh, it's great, Dad. I get so much satisfaction from directing the plays at church."

Times like this with her dad were a special treat for her. She'd spent lonely hours as a girl, longing for the attention of her absentee father. He'd learned and matured as much as she had.

When they finished their sandwiches, Dad retrieved the cookie jar from the counter. "I saw Nathan West in town the other day. I wondered what his business was."

Katie bit her lip and took a deep breath. Should she tell him the truth? "I've seen him. He's friends with Derek Hall." She avoided her father's eyes by taking a cookie from the jar and biting into it.

Her father frowned. "Is there a problem?" Her father, as a lawyer, had much experience reading people's body language.

Raising her gaze to meet his, she shook her head. "No, not really. He just wants us to get back together."

He pressed his lips together.

Katie laid her hand on his arm. "No, Dad, I told him no. I have no romantic interest in him, and I said so." But had Nathan really heard her?

"That's good. If there's a problem, let me know."

Her father could be intimidating. He'd had a lot of practice as a trial lawyer.

"I can handle it, Dad. I'm older, and Nathan is different too. But I'll let you know if I need your help."

Time to tell Dad about Jackson. She finished her cookie and leaned forward, her arms on the table. "There is something I need to tell you. It's not a secret, but I don't want you to think I'm trying to hide something from you."

Dad folded his arms and kept his face neutral. He was listening, and this encouraged her to continue.

"I've been seeing someone. His name is Jackson Stone. I met him in college, and his grandfather is a resident of the Senior Home."

"Did he go on the hayride with you?"

"Yes, he did. Why do you ask?"

He shrugged. "Someone said something. I expect you'll introduce him soon to your mother and me."

"I hope to. Only ... I told him about the baby—"

"And he's not interested in you anymore." Was it anger or disappointment in his voice and expression? Katie couldn't tell.

She hurried to contradict him. "No, Dad, it's not like that. I asked him to take a week to pray about it, to be sure that he won't ever hold it against me if our relationship should go forward." She sat back and tapped her fingers on the table. "The week is up on Sunday."

Her father pushed back his chair and snapped his fingers to call Chloe to him. He picked her up, and she curled up on his lap, purring contentedly as he stroked her back.

"Your mother and I are praying that you'll find a young man worthy of you." He held up his hand when she tried to interrupt. "No, let me finish."

Katie clamped her lips together, though she longed to speak out.

"If I'd been the father I should have been, and if your mother and I had been here for you, you may not have felt such a need to give in to Nathan's invitation. You had a baby, but I watched you the whole time. You grew and learned and matured through the experience. I know it broke your heart to give him away, but you did what you knew was best for him."

She nodded, tears in her eyes. She needed to hear this from

her father, even after six years. Every girl needed encouragement from her father.

"You're my daughter and a very special young woman. You give yourself so selflessly to others and to God. You deserve a man who will cherish and protect you, love you, and be at your side through thick and thin. If this Jackson is a man like that, I'll have no problem."

Katie stood up and walked around the table to put her arms around her father's neck. "Thank you, Daddy," she whispered. She straightened and stood at his side, her hand on his shoulder. "I believe Jackson is such a man. But I wanted to be fair to him and not keep secrets."

"That's wise, I think." Her father stood and began to clear the table. An indignant Chloe made them laugh as she stalked away after she'd been unceremoniously disturbed from her nap. Katie joined him in cleaning the kitchen, and within a few minutes, they were done.

"I have to work tonight, so I'll say goodbye to Chloe and be on my way. Thanks for lunch, Dad. And I'll let you know how things go with Jackson. I know you'll like him."

Would Jackson be back Sunday? He had to be, or her heart would break.

As she walked home, she checked her phone. Jackson had texted her that his grandfather had been admitted with a mild stroke. The family had to decide what to do after he got out of the hospital.

Would David return to the Senior Home? If not, she and Mary would miss him. And without his grandfather there, would she see less of Jackson?

13

Katie examined her pale, tired reflection in the mirror and yawned. She didn't mind the night shift, but the hours of missed sleep were beginning to tell. She tried to stuff too much living between shifts at the Senior Home, and the week hadn't been the easiest one of her life.

Would Jackson be in church this morning?

Father God, I want so much for Jackson to be there. He's a good man. I think I love him. I know You love me and want the best for me. I want Your will, but I'm worried that Your will isn't the same as mine. Forgive me and help me to trust You.

Makeup brightened her complexion. Satisfied with her choice of a dark blue dress with a black embroidered design around the neckline, she pulled her hair back from her face with a barrette and allowed her curls to cascade down her back.

Jackson's car wasn't in the parking lot, and she nearly cried when she didn't see him in the church. Haleigh turned and waved to her from where she sat with the Whites. Katie looked around and spotted her parents. They saw her and moved over so she could sit next to them as the prelude music began.

Her father leaned toward her and whispered, "Your friend didn't come?"

Katie looked over her shoulder, willing him to walk through the door. "Not yet."

Dad put his arm around her shoulders and squeezed.

As the congregation rose for the singing of the opening hymn, Katie blinked back tears of disappointment. No Jackson. Swallowing hard and taking a deep breath, she joined in the singing. "Joyful, joyful, we adore Thee, God of glory, Lord of love …"

A touch on her elbow startled her. She pivoted her head and looked up into Jackson's smiling face. Katie's breath caught, and tears filled her eyes. Mom and Dad moved over to make room for him, and her father winked at her.

Katie's heart sang before she could clear the tightness in her throat to sing the hymn again, praising God for His goodness.

Jackson came. He kept his promise to stay.

He laced his fingers with hers, and she might never let go. Her parents beside her looked straight ahead, but she could see they smiled.

The warmth of his hand traveled up her arm, and she breathed in the scent of his aftershave. Katie didn't remember much about the service or the pastor's message that day. Her usual detailed notes on the sermon were rather sketchy. She daydreamed about her future with Jackson.

"HI, CHERYL," Katie greeted the young blonde woman as she entered the bank Monday morning. She hadn't seen Cheryl Nelson since that day in her apartment.

"Oh, Katie, hi!" Cheryl hesitated as though she had more to say.

Katie's turn came next at the cashier's window, so they didn't have time for more conversation. When Katie turned to leave, Cheryl, who had waited, held the door open for her and fell into step beside her.

Cheryl glowed. The wan, depressed Cheryl that Katie had talked to a month ago had become her usual bubbly, attractive self.

"Katie, I want to thank you for talking to me that day. You don't know what it meant to me."

"You looked like you needed a friend or at least a listening ear. I'm glad I could help."

"I went home and talked to Lars. He finally understood that I just couldn't kill my ... our baby. He's actually excited now about being a father. Then he suggested that since we were planning to get married next year anyway, we should get married right away." The young woman's eyes sparkled, and her royal blue winter coat brought out the color of her eyes. "Will you come to our wedding? It's on Christmas Eve."

Katie sent a silent thanks to heaven. "I'm so glad you decided to keep your baby and that Lars didn't force you to choose between him and the baby. And congratulations about your wedding." She hadn't responded to the invitation yet. "Christmas Eve is a lovely time for a wedding. Will you have it in church?" Most churches in the area, including Greenlawn Bible, had services on Christmas Eve.

Cheryl shook her head. "No, Mom and Dad have rented their country club in Waverly." She sighed. "I have always dreamed of a big wedding, with all the trimmings, so to speak. But we decided on a smaller, more intimate ceremony and reception, with just relatives and a few close friends."

Katie nodded. "That sounds nice. I appreciate your invitation, but I'm scheduled to work on Christmas Eve." She'd turned down Jackson's invitation to spend Christmas Eve with his family too.

The smile disappeared from Cheryl's face momentarily. "Oh." She smiled again. "Well, I'll send you an invitation anyway. That way you'll have all the information just in case your schedule changes. And you may bring a friend if you wish."

Katie laid her hand on Cheryl's arm. "It means a lot to me

that you invited me to your wedding, even though I don't think I can come. And I'm glad to know I helped you that day."

"I've been reading that little book you gave me. It has made me think about my relationship with God. Lars and I have talked about going to church more regularly once we're married."

"I hope you do. I'll look for you there."

KATIE HAD READ Jesse White's homesickness in his first letter, although he expressed enthusiasm for his training and the people working with him. She responded with a newsy letter about home happenings. Planning to write to him again before going to work that evening, she first walked to her parents' house to check on supplies for Chloe.

A light covering of snow lay on the ground. Katie breathed in the crisp, early December air, glad for her warm coat and boots. Only two weeks before the Christmas play. She went over a to-do list in her mind, satisfied that they were right on schedule in their preparations.

The young adult Christmas party would be held the next Friday. The whole month would bring many visitors to the Senior Home, as relatives visited loved ones. Scouts and the 4-H club planned to sing Christmas carols, and the elementary department of Greenlawn Bible Church scheduled a play performance. The staff planned a party for the residents, and the program director had asked Katie to find a couple of simple games they could play.

Katie knew she'd be tired with all the festive activities, but she loved this time of year, especially as it related to the real reason to celebrate—Christ's birth. She regretted she couldn't spend as much time with Jackson as she had hoped. With his job and visiting his grandfather in rehab as well as her activities, they had to be satisfied with phone calls and texting.

She knocked on the back door of her parents' home, then opened it.

Katie breathed in the scent. "Mm, gingerbread." Several dozen of her mother's gingerbread men lay on one countertop, waiting to be decorated. Some of her earliest memories centered on her mother's specially decorated Christmas cookies, a treat for anyone who received them as a gift and for her family.

Mom and Dad's voices came from the living room as Chloe glided into the kitchen to greet her. Katie slipped off her boots at the door and hung her coat on the back of a kitchen chair, then she lifted Chloe and cuddled her in her arms.

"Hey, kitty, how are you today?" Chloe stared at her with blue eyes.

In the living room, Mom and Dad sat in their matching lounge chairs.

"Hi, Mom. Hi, Dad." She kissed each one's cheek in greeting. "I've come to check out Chloe's supplies."

They greeted her, but the telephone rang before they could start a conversation. Katie went to the kitchen to inspect cat supplies, the purring Chloe in her arms.

Her mother answered the phone, and Katie couldn't help hearing her end of the conversation. "Good morning, Annette ... What's that? ... Oh, no! I'm sorry.... How bad is it? ... I see. Is there anything we can do? ... Of course, we'll pray. Do you want me to come over? ... I understand. Annette, God will take care of him ... Yes, goodbye."

When Katie reentered the living room, her father had his arm around her very pale mother. "It's Jesse," Mom choked out. "There's been an accident."

Alarmed, Katie hurried across the room. "What's the matter with Jesse? Is he hurt?"

"Why don't you sit down, Gail." Dad gently guided Mom over to the sofa.

Katie knelt on the floor in front of her seated parents. Dad gently stroked Mom's back to calm her trembling.

"Jesse's been in a training accident of some sort. He's hurt, but they don't know the extent of his injuries. Annette and Jim are talking about flying out to be with him."

"Oh, Mom!" Katie sobbed, laying her head on her mother's knees. A vision of fun-loving Jesse White lying unconscious in a hospital bed attached to tubes and machines sent a chill through her. She tried to block her medical knowledge from dwelling on negative possibilities.

Her father's soothing baritone broke through their sobs. "Our gracious and good heavenly Father, we come to You on behalf of Jesse and the whole White family. We pray for Jesse's recovery and that he'll know Your comfort and peace at this critical time. Give the doctors skill and understanding as they treat him.

"We pray for our friends, Annette and Jim, who have received this terrible news. Guide their thoughts and their steps and help them in the decisions they have to make. And for the rest of the family, help them to trust and rest in You. In Jesus' name, amen."

Once she had control of her emotions, Katie got up. She knew Dad would take care of Mom, but her thoughts went to Haleigh and the Whites. Her friend might need her. Although engaged to Willie, Haleigh considered Jesse a dear friend, her *little brother*, as Katie did.

She hurried to Floral Creations, where Tia stood at the cash register.

"Good morning, Tia. Is Haleigh here?"

"Did you hear the news?" Tia looked ready to cry.

Katie nodded. "Isn't it terrible?"

Without replying, Tia waved a hand to indicate where Haleigh was helping a customer.

Haleigh had struggled in the past with the pain of loss. How would she handle the possibility of Jesse's death? *No one said Jesse died.* Katie didn't know exactly what she would say or do, but she'd come to be with Haleigh.

Waiting nearby, she looked at the floral displays until Haleigh finished. When the customer left, Haleigh turned to her. Except for her trembling hands and the strain on her face, she seemed surprisingly calm.

"You must have heard. I thought you might come." They held each other for a minute.

"Mrs. White called my mother while I was there."

"Thank you for coming." Haleigh's voice sounded thick, probably from crying. "I sent Willie home to be with his mom and dad. I told him Tia and I could handle the shop. He left reluctantly because we've been so busy, but family won out."

"As it should," Katie said. "You don't have any customers here right now, so would you like me to pray with you?"

"Please do."

Tia slipped out from behind the counter. "May I join you?" Katie raised her eyebrows in surprise that Tia expressed a sincere desire to be a part of their prayer time.

Haleigh held out her hand. "Of course."

The three young women held hands in a circle as Katie prayed first and then Haleigh.

"Amen," Tia said when they finished. "Do you think it will work? I mean, praying. Jesse's, um, a nice guy. He doesn't deserve this. Since he's a Christian, why would God do this to Him?"

Haleigh shook her head and sighed, tears streaking her face. "God doesn't have to tell us why. But sometimes it's hard to understand and accept what He allows to happen." She pulled a tissue out of her pocket to wipe her face and blow her nose.

Katie laid her hand on Tia's shoulder. "I believe God heard our prayer for Jesse, but I don't know how He'll answer." It felt surreal to think of Jesse in a hospital bed, perhaps broken and bleeding when only a few short weeks ago, they had talked together at the café. "How soon do you expect more news, Haleigh?"

Haleigh shrugged. "I'm not sure. Willie's parents are making arrangements to go out there as soon as they know more."

The door opened with a jingle, and Tia scooted back to the cash register. Katie squeezed Haleigh's hand and whispered, "See you later."

As she walked out the door, Katie said hello to the customer entering, an acquaintance from town. As the door closed behind her, the customer said, "I've heard rumors about Jesse White being in an accident." Poor Haleigh would probably be responding to curious customers like that all day.

Katie needed sleep before reporting for work that evening, but Jesse remained uppermost in her mind. *Father God, please make him all right.* If Jim and Annette White flew out to be with Jesse, would they be home for Christmas? Would Jesse come home to recover?

She wrote the letter to Jesse she'd been planning to write, keeping it newsy and upbeat, not dwelling on his accident, but wishing him a speedy recovery. She'd wait to mail it. If he came home, she'd give it to him.

She wanted to talk to Jackson, but he couldn't receive calls at this time of the day.

Her busy mind kept her tired body from sleeping, different scenarios with Jesse invading her sphere. She finally managed a couple hours of restful sleep.

At work during the night, she prayed for her friend many times. Haleigh texted her to tell her that Greenlawn Bible Church held a prayer vigil for Jesse that evening, starting at seven and going as long as people wanted to pray. Katie wished she could be there.

JACKSON INHALED as he exited the school building and coughed from the bite in the December air. The buses had left an hour ago to take students home, although a group of students talked in the parking lot. Vehicles still filled the faculty lot.

The recent light snowfall made him long for the ski slopes. Did Katie ski? He hoped so.

So much needed to be done before holiday break and the semester's end. He felt a little overwhelmed.

When Grandpa Stone got out of rehab, he'd come to the farm for a few days. That meant his family expected Jackson home more often to help with Grandpa's care. He didn't mind because of his love for Grandpa, but he regretted the loss of time with Katie just as they had reached firmer ground in their relationship.

The musical tones of his cell phone indicated a call. Katie. He closed his eyes and smiled.

"Hello."

"Hi, Jackson. How was your day?"

The sound of her voice released tension from his shoulders. "Well, so-so."

"Problems?"

"No, just a lot to do before holiday break." He ran his fingers through his hair. "But it's good to hear your voice. I've been thinking about you."

"You have?" She sounded pleased. "That's nice."

"It would be nicer if I could see you."

"I know. I feel the same way. Are you coming to Greenlawn on Sunday?"

"That's the plan. Texting and phone calls are fine but seeing you would be even better."

"I agree." Katie paused. Jackson waited because he sensed she had something on her mind. "Jackson, we've had some sad news. I would have called yesterday, but, well, the Whites, you know, Willie's family, learned yesterday that Willie's younger brother, Jesse, had a terrible accident."

"Jesse's the one in the Air Force, right? What happened?" He'd never met Jesse.

"He was involved in a training accident yesterday morning.

The doctors are still evaluating his injuries." Her voice held worry. She must be hurting for her friend.

"Is it bad?"

"Bad enough. A couple of broken ribs, a broken leg, bruises. His parents are flying out to see him, and they hope to bring him home if he's able to travel. He had only a couple more weeks of basic training." Her voice thickened. "Jesse was always so full of life and fun. He had so much energy, always had to be doing something. And he looked forward to joining the Air Force for so long. He had his pilot's license and loved to fly."

If Jackson didn't have a faculty meeting this afternoon and twenty student homework papers to correct before tomorrow, he would drive to Greenlawn now. "Are you working tonight?"

"Yes. I got up just a few minutes ago. I wanted you to know about Jesse so you could pray for him. Will you?"

Jealousy tweaked Jackson at the pleading tone in her voice. This guy was really special to her. "Of course I will."

"Thank you." He heard the relief in her voice. "How's your grandfather? I miss him."

"Grandpa's doing well in rehab, and we expect to bring him home to the farm for a couple of days before he returns to Greenlawn." He checked his watch and turned to go back into the building. "I have to go. There's a faculty meeting in two minutes, and I have to be there."

"Okay. I'm looking forward to Sunday. Mom and Dad have invited us to go out to eat with them after church. Is that all right with you?"

The soft appeal in her voice made his heart thud. How could he refuse her invitation? Her parents probably wanted to check him out, to judge whether he was right for their daughter. "That's fine with me, as long as I'm with you. Let me know if there's any more news about your friend."

He rushed into the cafeteria just as the meeting began.

14

"*I*'ve never seen Willie so shaken." Haleigh unwrapped a package of disposable plates decorated with poinsettias. "He wanted to go with his parents, and he would have if we weren't so busy at the shop."

When Haleigh returned to Greenlawn last May, she took up residence in the Sousa family's log home to care for it while they were away on sabbatical. Katie came to the cabin often to spend time with her friend. Now she worked with Haleigh to prepare for the young adult Christmas party to be held here that evening.

"The Whites are a close-knit family." Katie folded the last of the napkins and arranged them on the dining room table. "The news shook up the entire town. After all, Jesse is one of our own."

"Willie said the idea of his brother dying seemed unreal, just like when Aubrey had her accident." Haleigh emptied two bags of chips into big bowls. "I can't imagine Jesse staying in bed or limping around on crutches. He's a man of action, more so than even Willie."

Katie placed the punch bowl at one end of the dining room table. "Thank God we won't be attending a funeral. But with a possible concussion, broken ribs, and a fractured femur, it will probably be a couple of months at least before he'll be able to do much." She shook her head and smiled. "Maybe it will be time for the Three Sisters to get back into action mode."

If she, Aubrey, and Haleigh put their heads together, they might come up with a way to help Jesse.

"Maybe." Haleigh shifted the position of a stack of napkins. "The Whites plan to celebrate the new year in Greenlawn, so Aubrey and Jeremy will be in town." She handed Katie a package of paper cups. "Willie's parents say that Jesse isn't himself. He's angry and questions why God would allow the accident. He's in a lot of pain. They hope he'll feel better by the time they bring him home."

Katie removed the wrapper from the cups and arranged them beside the punch bowl. She had seen for herself that active men like Jesse often became difficult patients.

Haleigh stepped back and looked around. "I think that's it until everybody comes with their food." She straightened a crooked red taper on the table.

"You did a wonderful job of decorating. It's beautiful! This place is perfect for our party." The living room and dining room glowed with red poinsettias, garlands of evergreen, multi-colored lights, and a Christmas tree decorated from top to bottom with lights, ornaments, and tinsel garland.

"Thank you. I had a lot of fun doing it. It helps to have a fiancé who's a florist. And thank you for all your help. I'm glad you didn't have to work today."

"Me too. I only wish Jackson could come, but he has to take his brother and sister Christmas caroling with their church. His parents have some business to take care of with Jackson's grandfather. His mother was rather insistent."

"I'm sorry, Katie. Things aren't working out for you two to have time together right now. I like Jackson a lot, and it would be fun to have him here tonight."

Katie nodded and sighed. "I know." She walked over to the

CD player. "May I turn on the Christmas music? People should start arriving soon."

"Go ahead and push the button. It's ready to play."

Just then, Katie heard voices outside, steps on the porch, and the doorbell rang.

Haleigh opened the door with a smile. "Welcome. Come on in," she said.

Later, accompanied by Pastor Pete on his guitar, Doug on his banjo, and Courtney on her mandolin, everyone gathered in the living room, some on the sofa and chairs, some on the floor, to sing Christmas carols. The Christmas lights, the only lights that remained on, filled the room with a holiday glow.

Katie never tired of singing the traditional carols, and she loved many of the newer songs as well. She sighed in contentment. If only Jackson was here.

As the group exuberantly sang, "Glo-o-o-o-ria, in excelsis deo," Katie heard the doorbell ring. Sitting closer to the door than Haleigh, she looked at her friend with raised eyebrows. When Haleigh nodded, Katie stood, walked to the door, and opened it.

"Jackson!"

"Hello, Katie. Am I too late for the party?"

He looked good with a knit cap on his head and his cheeks and nose rosy from the nippy air. His eyes reflected the icicle lights strung along the porch.

"You came." She grabbed his hand, pulled him inside, and closed the door behind him. Several of the young adults called out greetings to him as the song ended. He handed her his coat, and she laid it on the bed in one of the rooms as he waited by the door for her to return.

Haleigh grinned at them. "We didn't expect to see you tonight, Jackson."

"I got off for good behavior." He rubbed his hands together and smiled at Katie. "My parents came home in time for refreshments and took the kids off my hands, so I came here."

He sat down on the floor beside Katie and took her hand. "That was good singing, I heard. What's the next song?"

As the musicians strummed their instruments, the group sang, "Go, Tell It on the Mountain."

Her fingers entwined with Jackson's, their shoulders touching, Katie gazed into his eyes. Her heart overflowed with joy. Jackson came!

AFTER WORKING three twelve-hour shifts on Christmas Eve, Christmas, and the following night, Katie headed for the White home to visit Jesse for the first time since he returned home on Christmas Eve.

Her strength reserves nearly depleted, she needed the three days off that followed. Her pre-Christmas activities had been fun and rewarding, but she had pushed herself to her physical limits. Working the last three nights had allowed her coworkers with families to have the time off. Now it was her turn. Visiting Jesse headed her list of things to do, and she'd brought Chloe along for reinforcement.

Annette White greeted her warmly and welcomed her into the house. Setting down the cat carrier, Katie removed her boots and placed them on the mat by the front door. She hung her coat on the coat tree, just like old times.

"I'm glad to see you, Katie. How was your Christmas?"

"Very busy, but enjoyable."

"We were sorry to miss your Christmas play."

"Someone recorded it. If you're interested, I can probably get you a copy."

"I'd like that. Thank you. I hope ... well, maybe Jesse will want to watch it too." Chloe mewed, and Mrs. White gestured toward the cat carrier. "Who do we have here?"

Katie unlatched the door and lifted out the kitten. "I guess you haven't met Chloe yet. She was left outside the apartment house a couple of months ago. She lives with my parents because I can't have a cat in my apartment, but she goes visiting with me. I take her to the Senior Home on my days off. The residents love her."

Mrs. White gently scratched behind Chloe's ear. The cat purred. "She has such beautiful markings."

"Yes, I love the pattern of the black stripes on her silver fur. I hope it's all right that I brought her. I thought she might brighten Jesse's day."

The older woman shook her head. "I don't mind at all. Especially if she can help my son. But Sweetie Pie might take exception to having another cat in the house."

Sweetie Pie, the Whites' calico, held princess status in the household—at least, the cat thought so.

The prominent lines around Mrs. White's mouth and the dark circles under her eyes revealed her stress, even though she smiled. Katie laid her hand on the older woman's arm. "How is Jesse?"

Tears filled her eyes, and her voice wobbled. "He's ... well ... he's doing all right, I guess. They let him come home. The trip was hard on him, and he has to go for evaluation and rehab in a couple of weeks. It's just that ... he's not Jesse."

"I'm so sorry this happened to him. It must be hard to keep him down." Bottling up Jesse's restless energy would be difficult.

"On the contrary, he doesn't seem interested in much right now. The doctor at the base hospital said he's healing, but it will take time for him to be active again." Mrs. White folded her arms in front of her and hunched her shoulders as though chilled. "We've set up the dining room as a temporary bedroom for him. I'll let him know you're here."

Katie followed her into the living room. Mrs. White knocked on the partly open door and entered while Katie waited on the living room sofa with Chloe in her lap.

"You have a visitor."

"I'd rather not." The voice didn't sound like Jesse's. "I'm not up to having company right now."

After a slight pause, his mother said, "I can send her away if that's what you want. I'm sure she'll understand. But I thought you'd like to see Katie."

"Katie Mann?"

Mrs. White laughed. "Is there another?"

The rustling of movement came from the room. Chloe suddenly jumped out of Katie's arms, startling her, and trotted through the doorway, her ears pricked forward, her tail upright.

"Whoa, who's this?" Jesse exclaimed.

"This is Katie's cat, Chloe. Shall I send Katie in?" Mrs. White appeared in the doorway. "Chloe's a sensation," she whispered with a smile. "You can go in now," she said in her normal voice.

Sweetie Pie stalked out through the doorway and scooted up the stairs.

Katie chuckled as she stood. "I guess you were right about your cat's reaction to Chloe."

"She'll get over it." Mrs. White motioned for Katie to go in.

Walking quietly into the dining room, she took in the scene before Jesse noticed her. Chloe lay cat-fashion on Jesse's stomach, purring loudly, her tail twitching periodically, as he lay propped up by pillows in his hospital bed. Jesse gently stroked the cat's back.

He'd lost some weight, and a bruise spread across the side of his head. Katie had seen worse in the emergency room during nurse's training, but this was her friend, Jesse. She fought to keep back the tears.

Clearing her throat, she strode forward. "Well, I see Chloe has you figured out."

He turned his head. His smile didn't quite reach his eyes. "Hi."

"So, how are you doing today?" she said in her best nurse's voice.

He shrugged. "I've been better."

She bent to kiss his cheek. When she laid her hand on top of his, he grasped hers and held on tightly. Chloe moved to his side and curled up.

"Is there much pain, Jesse?"

"Naw." He looked away.

"Jesse?" She could read it in his eyes and in the rigidity of his body.

"Sometimes." He moaned. "I thought the pain would be mostly gone by now."

It broke her heart to see him so weak and vulnerable. She decided not to discuss his injuries unless he wanted to. Sliding her hand out of his, she pulled a chair over next to the bed. "Willie and Haleigh are due back today, aren't they?"

"Yes, and Aubrey and Jeremy are going to stop by on their way back to the seminary." Jesse shifted slightly, and his face brightened. A safe subject, Katie decided.

"Willie had a good season at Floral Creations. And their house will be ready in another month or so." She tried to think of some other community news that might interest him. "Lars and Cheryl were married on Christmas Eve."

"I didn't know they had set a date." Jesse stroked the sleeping Chloe at his side. "I figured they would have a big society wedding."

Katie didn't offer a response to his statement. "Derek Hall has changed so much. He's involved in church, and he seems to be trying to make up for his past."

"Really?"

Chloe stood and sniffed Jesse's chin. He chuckled. "You silly cat, you're tickling me." She climbed back on his stomach and sat, staring at him. He tipped his head down to look at her. "Her eyes are an unusual blue-green." He glanced at Katie. "I think she's trying to read my mind."

Happy that Chloe seemed to be raising Jesse's spirits, Katie said, "Chloe wants to know you're okay, Jess."

He stroked the cat. "Not yet, kitty. Maybe one day soon." His eyes didn't hold their usual sparkle. "How's the nursing going?"

She smiled. "I love it, Jesse. I love the residents at the Senior Home."

"Do you think you'll be there for a while?"

She shrugged. "If that's where God wants me." A shadow passed across her friend's face, and he looked away. "The Senior Home is a good place to work, and Greenlawn is a wonderful place to live."

She pulled on a curl. She hadn't told anyone, not even Jackson or Haleigh, what she would tell Jesse now. "I'd really like to go into pediatric nursing. And I think the Lord is calling me to the mission field. There are a lot of opportunities with medical missions."

He didn't respond right away. He stroked Chloe as he stared at nothing. Then he shook his head "Red, do you really believe God guides you, tells you where to go and what to do?"

She nodded. "I do."

He frowned. "So, tell me this. I believed God directed me to join the Air Force. And now, look at me. I'm a cripple!" He whacked the mattress with the palm of his hand. "Can't do much of anything. I didn't even finish basic training. Where does that leave me? Why did God do this to me?" A sob shook his body, and tears filled his eyes. He swiped his eyes with the back of his hand.

Chloe moved up to his chest and sniffed his face again. He kept his gaze turned away, his hands lying idly on top of his blanket. Chloe crouched down and waited.

Compassion for her suffering friend filled Katie. "I don't know, Jess. I wish I had answers. What could she say that might comfort him? "My trouble came because I didn't follow God's way, yours when you did." She sighed. "I think God just wants us to move on."

She stood and placed the chair back. "Jesse, as a nurse, I'm saying be patient, healing will come. As your friend, I want you to know I'm praying for you. Remember the verse we shared before you left?" She assumed his silence meant assent. "Isaiah 41:10 is a promise that God will strengthen and help us. Try to believe that."

As she reached over to pick up Chloe, Jesse grabbed her hand. "It's so hard, Red."

She squeezed his hand. "I know." She lifted her cat. "Now you need to rest so you'll be able to enjoy your other company later."

"Will you come back?" The pleading in his voice touched her heart.

"Of course, but not today. Get well."

A spark of hope appeared in his eyes, and he released her hand. Chloe watched him over her shoulder as they exited.

Jesse faced a long road to recovery. A visit with his brother and sister would be good for him. Having been through a similar time of trauma, Aubrey could encourage him in his recovery. Willie's patience and solid faith could help rebuild Jesse's weakened faith. And prayer, always prayer, would lead to healing of his body and soul.

Katie arrived at her apartment with enough energy to fix and drink a cup of tea. She lay down on the sofa, finding a comfortable position for a pillow under her head, and pulled a fleece blanket over her. "Time for a winter's nap," she sighed as she sank back.

15

*D*ing.

What was that? Where was she? Katie struggled to wake up. Oh, someone rang her doorbell. She blinked and sat up, pushing the blanket to the floor. The doorbell rang again, followed by a knock.

"Okay, I'm coming," she called out, staggering to her feet. When she glanced at the wall clock, her eyes widened. She'd napped for three hours.

Through the peephole, she saw Haleigh on the other side. She opened the door.

"I almost thought you weren't home." Haleigh walked in.

"I'm here." Katie yawned. "Wow, did I sleep!"

"Are you okay? I can come back another time."

Katie ran her fingers through her hair and stepped back. "No, no. Please come in. I think my busy life is catching up with me."

She led Haleigh into the living room, and they sat on the sofa.

"I wanted to show you some pictures of my new nephew. Have you seen the ones I put on Facebook?" Haleigh pulled an envelope out of her coat pocket.

Katie shook her head and tried to push her curls into order. "I haven't been on Facebook recently. I've been too busy."

"Good. I get to introduce you to Jonathan Luke Abbott." She handed several photos to Katie.

"He's beautiful! They look happy."

"He's so sweet. Jason and Carmella are so happy and proud. I hope they'll be able to come to Greenlawn for a weekend soon. Then you'll get to see for yourself how cute he is."

Katie handed the photos back. "How do your mom and dad feel about being grandparents?"

"They're so excited. Mom said they had trouble keeping within their Christmas budget this year. She had to keep reminding Dad that Jonathan is only one month old. He didn't need a baseball glove or a fishing pole yet." They laughed together.

As she tucked the envelope of photographs back into her pocket, Haleigh's expression sobered. "We went to the Whites' house as soon as we got into town to see Jesse. Aubrey and Jeremy will stop by on their way home." She shook her head. "Poor Jesse."

Katie nodded. "I saw him earlier today. I think having Willie and Aubrey visit will help cheer him up."

"I hope so. I left Willie there and came here to see you." She bit her lip. "I think I needed a little time to get away and process the changes." Tears pooled in her eyes.

"I know what you mean." Katie put her arm around her friend's shoulders. "Jesse needs all the encouragement possible right now. He's got a long road to recovery."

"I guess we all thought of the risks if he had deployed to a war zone, but we didn't think about him getting hurt like this during training. His mom and dad are tired and worried, but they say the doctors indicated he'd recover."

"I took Chloe when I visited him." Katie smiled as she dropped her arm.

Haleigh's face brightened. "What did Jesse think?"

"She just poured on the charm, and I think he fell for it. She seems to be quite sensitive to people who are sick or in pain. I'm going to take her again when I visit him."

Haleigh leaned forward, resting her arms on her knees. "That's how Sunshine was." She wrapped her arms around her abdomen. "I still miss my dog."

"Do you think you'll get another one?"

Haleigh shrugged. "Probably. Willie and I have talked about it. We decided to wait until spring or summer to decide, after the wedding, when we're settled in our house."

Katie yawned. "I'm sorry." She giggled.

Haleigh stood. "I didn't know I was that boring." She smiled and buttoned her coat. "I'd better get back to Willie and let you go back to bed." She walked to the door, Katie right behind her.

Katie yawned again and stood by the door as Haleigh went out. "I've never been so glad for a day off. Jackson's supposed to call sometime."

"You're always caring for others. You need some time for yourself. Tell Jackson hi for me." Haleigh lifted her hand and waved then turned toward the stairway.

Katie's head ached and her stomach growled, reminding her that she hadn't eaten much today. She took a container of yogurt out of her refrigerator. She also cut up a banana and made herself another cup of tea. After eating, she took a shower and dressed. Returning to her sofa, she cuddled under the blanket, wishing for Chloe to cuddle with her.

She dozed off. A sudden knock on her door made her jump. Moaning softly, she shuffled to the door.

Through the peephole, Katie recognized the man holding flowers on the other side of the door as a part-time employee from Floral Creations. She opened the door.

"Flowers for Katie Mann."

"That's me." She held out her hands, and he gave them to her. Jackson sent her flowers again.

"Thank you." She raised the bouquet of mixed-cut flowers to

her nose. "Wait a minute!" She had a bad feeling. She thrust the flowers back at the confused delivery person and removed a small envelope from the bouquet. She read the enclosed card.

Just what she thought. Nathan again!

She tucked the card back into the envelope and pushed it into the bouquet. "I'm sorry, I can't accept these. Take them back."

"What? I can't do that."

"Yes, you can. Just tell Will or Haleigh I can't accept them. They'll know what to do."

"Oh. I don't know." The young man frowned.

"Really, it's okay. Just a minute." Leaving the door open, Katie hurried over to her purse on the coffee table and grabbed a five-dollar bill out of it. "Here, this is for your trouble." She handed him the money and wondered whether to call it a tip or a bribe.

He hesitated, then took it. "Thank you, I think."

"Look, if they have any questions, tell them to call me. They know my number."

He nodded and left with the flowers.

Katie shut her door and leaned against it. That poor guy. She hoped he wouldn't quit his job after meeting this crazy woman, but she had to stop Nathan somehow. He didn't seem to understand the word *no*.

Turning on a CD of soft classical music, Katie sat on the sofa, wondering when Jackson would call. Or maybe she should call him.

She knew she should do something, but she continued to sit listlessly on the sofa, dozing.

When her cell phone rang, she leaned forward to pick it up. It slipped from her fingers, but she caught it before it fell to the floor.

Her mind fuzzy with sleep, she didn't think to check out who called. "Hello."

"Hello, Miss Kate. How are you this fine afternoon?"

"Hi, Jackson." The sound of his voice sent zings through her. "I've been waiting for your call." She yawned and stretched.

"What's this? Am I making you yawn, I'm that boring?"

"No, I'm just tired, that's all."

"Oh, I guess you don't feel like going out for hot chocolate and a stroll tonight." He sounded disappointed.

She had to be honest. "I'd love to, but I'm so tired, I think I'd best stay in. Will tomorrow be all right? Can you come to Greenlawn tomorrow?"

"Are you okay?"

Katie nodded her head, although he couldn't see her. "Yes, but I've been so busy for the last month. Now I have some downtime, and I think my body is saying, *enough!*"

"If I come tomorrow, will you go with me to see Grandpa? We can stop and get Chloe. How about having lunch with me, and we'll spend the afternoon together? I don't have many days left before I have to go back to teaching, and then I'll be taking graduate courses as well."

"That will be great. And there's someone I would like you to meet."

"Oh?"

"You remember I told you about Willie White's brother, Jesse, who's in the Air Force?"

"Yes, I do. He got hurt, right?"

"He's suffering, Jackson. He's home now, and I'd like you to meet him. I took Chloe to see him earlier today."

Startled by a loud knock on her door, she said, "Just a minute." She got up and looked out her peephole. *Nathan!* He stood outside her door, frowning, with the bouquet of flowers in his hand. He knocked again, louder.

"Is everything all right, Katie?" Jackson sounded worried.

"Katie, I know you're there," Nathan shouted. "Open the door!"

She had no intention of doing that. She took a few steps back and said softly into the phone. "It's okay. I have three locks on my door."

"Is someone trying to get in? Call the police!"

She didn't really want to tell Jackson and get him involved, but he already knew about Nathan. "It's just Nathan. He sent me flowers, and I refused them. I think he's a little put out."

Nathan pounded on her door. "Katie!"

"Get someone to help you," Jackson shouted. She grimaced and moved the phone away from her ear.

She tried to keep her voice steady as her heart pounded. "He won't get in, and he won't hurt me." At least she hoped not.

A man's voice came from downstairs. "What are you doing, young man? Stop your noise, or I'm calling the police."

"I'm sorry," Nathan said. "Do you know if Katie Mann is home?"

"Can't say, but if I were her and at home, I wouldn't open the door for you. You sound like a lunatic."

"Sorry, sir," Nathan muttered.

Katie smiled despite her irritation. Dear Mr. Case lived in the apartment below her. She'd known the Cases for many years.

Nathan knocked again, more gently. "I know you're in there, Katie. I'm leaving the flowers out here. You had no right to send them back."

Katie didn't answer. With her ear pressed to the door, she listened as Nathan thumped down the stairs and the outside door closed. She didn't retrieve the flowers. She didn't want them.

She blew out a breath and raised the phone to her ear. "I'm okay, Jackson. He's gone."

"You sure? That guy sounds dangerous."

"I've never known him to be violent. Maybe a little pushy. You've met Nathan. He just won't take no for an answer. The night lock will be on the outside door in a few minutes. Then he won't be able to get in again tonight."

"If you say so."

"Mr. Case, who lives downstairs, threatened to call the police, so Nathan left." Time to change the subject. "I'll be glad to see you tomorrow."

"It's a date. If I come by about eleven, will that be all right?" He had calmed.

"Perfect." Wide awake now, she plopped back on the sofa and pulled the blanket over her. "Tell me about your day."

KATIE'S ASSURANCES that Nathan posed no danger to her didn't convince Jackson. Nathan seemed to think he had some kind of right to Katie and tried to harass her into accepting him.

Jackson decided to go to Greenlawn early and make sure that Nathan guy wasn't pestering his girl. He didn't view himself as a knight in shining armor, but he was ready to fight for her, to protect her, if necessary. One day soon, he'd ask Katie to marry him, and he figured this was his prerogative.

He picked up his coat to put it on when his phone rang. He smiled when he saw his mother's number on his phone. "Hi, Mom."

The smile left his face as he listened to her.

"I'm sorry, Mom. I can't do it today. I have other plans ... Tell you what, I'll take them to see Grandpa tomorrow ... That girl's name is Katie." Jackson sighed. "Yes, I plan to have you meet her. It just hasn't worked out yet ... I'm not a kid anymore, Mom. I love all of you, and I've spent a lot of time with you over Christmas break, but I need time to live my own life too ... Okay. See you tomorrow. Bye."

Jackson shook his head as he ended the call with his mother. She had to stop assuming he'd be available every time she needed a babysitter. His brother and sister weren't babies and could probably take care of themselves for the length of time Mom would be gone.

His family would love Katie as soon as they met her. He just knew it. Grandpa Stone had spoken well of her. But Jackson worried about his mother's attitude. She seemed to be having a hard time accepting the fact that he had a life apart from the rest of the family.

As he left his apartment and got in his SUV, a plan formed in his mind.

He stopped at the Hillside Diner for a cup of coffee and used up time walking around Greenlawn, looking in shop windows and exploring the streets. His breath came out in frosty puffs, and he left footprints in the coating of snow on the sidewalks.

Snow sat on tree branches like white blossoms, and Christmas lights and lawn ornaments decorated most homes. The shouts and laughter of children playing outside echoed in the air. He waved to some familiar faces, and he stopped at Floral Creations to say hi to Will and Haleigh. Thankfully, he didn't see any sign of Nathan West.

When he pulled up in front of Katie's apartment house, the sight of her outside putting finishing touches to a snowman nearly took his breath away. Her copper hair fell in soft curls to her shoulders beneath her pink knit hat. Her eyes sparkled, and her smile welcomed him. He hurried around his car toward her.

Splat! A snowball hit the middle of his chest. Giggling, she bent to pick up more snow. He moved too quickly for her and grabbed her around the waist before she could make another snowball.

"So, you like snow." He grinned as he looked from Katie to a pile of snow.

"No, no!" She laughed as she struggled to get away.

He let go of her, and she fell into the snow. She looked at him and then at the snow beside her. He smiled and reached out to help her up. She wouldn't try to pull him down, would she?

When she grabbed his hand, he hauled her to her feet and against him. She pushed away, and their eyes connected and held. He looked at her mouth, wanting to kiss her, but moving curtains in a couple of windows in the apartment house prevented him.

"Is that any way to greet a person?' He brushed the snow off her coat.

"Good morning, Jackson. If you had been a few minutes earlier, you could have had a part in my great snow masterpiece." She waved toward the snowman.

"We'll have to try again another time. I think I have a lunch date today with a certain Katie Mann." He gave a little bow.

She looked around. "Katie Mann? I'm Katie Mann. You mean you want to have lunch with me?" She pointed to herself with a snow-covered glove.

He nodded. "That's the plan."

She clapped her hands together to get rid of the snow. "I'd better check my social calendar." She pretended to take something out of her pocket. "Oh, yes, right here it says, "Lunch with one Jackson Stone." She pretended to return something to her pocket. "Are you Jackson Stone?"

"Yes, ma'am. That's me."

She looped her hand through his arm. "I'm glad. I'd be delighted to have lunch with you, Jackson Stone."

"Where would you like to eat, Miss Mann?"

"How about the café in town? They have a delicious lunch menu. Haleigh and I eat there often. And it's within walking distance if you don't mind the cold."

"What about going to see Grandpa later?"

"No problem. We can come back here and get your car. Then we can go to my parents' house, pick up Chloe, and go to the Senior Home."

"I guess you have it all planned out. Let's go."

"I'm good at planning." She pushed her curls back from her face.

"Oh, really? I like that—a planning woman." He smiled at her. "I have plans too." He wiggled his eyebrows.

He almost told her he planned to marry her but clamped his lips together. It was too soon to approach that subject. "I plan to take you to lunch, pick up Chloe, and go see Grandpa."

Katie shook her head. "You goof!" Did the color in her cheeks come from the cold air, or was she blushing?

16

*L*unch with Katie, a brief visit with her parents when they picked up Chloe, and a visit with Grandpa Stone and Mary Davis at the Senior Home—the afternoon with Katie was wonderful, but it whizzed by too fast for Jackson.

As they left the Senior Home, Katie said, "Remember I told you about Jesse White, Willie's brother? Will you go to see him with me?"

Jealousy twitched inside. Jackson nodded. "If you'd like, we can do that." He hoped he didn't sound as uncertain as he felt. He knew the wounded man to be someone special to the young woman beside him. He plucked the cat out of Katie's arms. "You say Chloe likes him?"

"Definitely."

"Well then, I guess it's okay. Chloe is a good judge of character."

Jackson placed Chloe in the carrier in the back seat. He closed the door and caught Katie watching him. "What?" Could she read his jealous thoughts?

She shook her head. "Never mind." Jackson opened the door for her, and she slid into the passenger seat.

He got behind the steering wheel and started the car. She

didn't look at him or say anything. Was she angry or lost in thought?

"Earth calling Katie." She jumped, then smiled. She didn't look angry. "You have to tell me how to get to the Whites' house."

"Oh, I'm sorry. It's not far." She told him where to turn.

As he pulled up and stopped in front of the house, he leaned against the steering wheel. "I have a favor to ask of you."

"Okay."

He tapped on the steering wheel. Reading uncertainty in her expression, he brushed her cheek with his gloved hand. "It's nothing bad. It's just that I told my mother I would bring Michael and Rebecca to see Grandpa tomorrow, and I'd like you to go with us."

She broke into a bright smile. "Oh, Jackson, I'd love to meet your brother and sister. I have tomorrow off. I'd be glad to go with you."

"And when I take them back, I'd like for you to go with us so you can meet my parents."

"But that will be a lot of extra driving for you."

He didn't think she'd object. "Well, if you'd rather not, that's okay. I thought it would be a good time for you to meet my family."

She grasped his arm. "I want to meet your family."

"Good." He patted her hand and opened his door. "Then we'll work something out."

He opened the car door for Katie and removed the cat carrier from the back seat. Katie introduced him to Mrs. White when she greeted them at the door, and she invited them in.

"It's a pleasure to meet you, Jackson." He shook her hand when she offered it.

"I'm glad to meet you, too, Mrs. White. Katie talks about your family a lot, and I've met Willie."

She pointed to the carrier in Jackson's hand. "I see you've

brought your USO entertainer again today. She was a big hit with the troops on her previous visit."

"Chloe does have a way about her." Jackson set the carrier down and let the cat out.

Without hesitation, Chloe bounded into the living room. "Hello, cat," they heard Jesse greet her from the other end of the room.

"Jesse's in the living room." Mrs. White spoke quietly. "He decided he wanted to get up for a while today. Willie and Haleigh came home yesterday, and Aubrey and Jeremy stopped by, which seemed to raise his spirits. Along with the visit from you and Chloe."

Katie and Jackson followed her into the living room. Jesse's large frame lay stretched out on his father's blue recliner, his right leg encased in a white cast. Chloe stood with her front paws against his chest, kneading and purring furiously as the big man stroked her. He looked up and smiled at Katie. His eyes widened when he saw Jackson beside her.

Katie leaned over and gave him a kiss on the cheek. "Hi, Jesse, I see you're up today. Feeling better?"

"It gets monotonous looking at the same pretty wallpaper day after day. I needed a change of scenery." He gave Jackson another look.

"Jackson Stone, I'd like you to meet Jesse White."

"Good to meet you, Jesse." Jackson hesitated, waiting to see if Jesse could shake hands. Jesse put out his right hand, and Jackson stepped forward to shake it, surprised by the wounded man's powerful grip. He saw the challenge in Jesse's eyes and understood its meaning. Did Katie know Jesse was in love with her? "I'm sorry about your accident, man. It's tough."

Jesse shrugged. "The doc says I'm getting better. Once the pain stops, maybe I'll think so too."

Jesse's mother came bustling in with a tray loaded with mugs of hot chocolate and Christmas cookies. "I was hoping for someone to help eat up these cookies, and hot chocolate's always good on a cold day. Unless you'd rather have coffee, Jackson." She set the tray on a small table next to Jesse.

"Thank you. Hot chocolate is fine."

Katie and Jesse added their thanks, and Mrs. White left the room.

"Did you have a good visit with Aubrey and Jeremy yesterday?" Katie handed mugs to the men.

Jesse blew on the steaming drink. "Yes, and they'll be back on New Year's Eve."

"Will Mike and Madison be coming?" Katie turned to Jackson. "Mike is the oldest of the White kids, and Madison is his wife."

"Yes. The whole family will be here for New Year's Day, as well as some of our other relatives. This was planned before my accident." Jesse frowned. "I almost wish they wouldn't come now."

Jackson sipped his hot chocolate. He wanted to encourage the hurting man, but he had never been immobilized like Jesse. He feared that Jesse might take anything he said as a challenge for Katie's attention.

"The White clan enjoys their get-togethers," Katie said, "and you always looked forward to them. Your family wants to see you. They need to know how you are. And you'll probably be glad to see them."

Jesse shrugged. "Maybe. I guess I can hide out in my room if necessary." He grimaced and shifted his body slightly, disturbing the dozing cat on his chest.

As they each chose a cookie from the tray, Chloe began sniffing. With a chuckle, Jesse broke off half of his Christmas tree and divided it into smaller pieces. He laid the pieces on the arm of his chair. Chloe sat with her tail curled around her, eating them.

Katie waggled her finger at him. "Uh-oh, Jess, you're spoiling her."

"Humor me. I need amusement," he murmured, a twinkle in

his eyes. He finished the other half of the cookie in two bites and reached for another. "Mom's sugar cookies are the best."

Katie shook her head. "Umm, Jesse, your mother didn't make these cookies."

Jesse stopped with a cookie almost in his mouth. "She didn't?"

Jackson bit his lip to keep from laughing at the expression on Jesse's face.

Katie wiped a crumb off her lip. "Nope. Haleigh and I had a cookie bake before the young adult Christmas party. We made lots and lots of cookies and gave some to your mother because we knew she had other things on her mind. In fact, we gave away lots of Christmas cookies. We were planning to send some to you until—" Katie stopped, her eyes big.

A shadow of emotion passed over Jesse's face. With his finger, he straightened Chloe's tail. She pulled it back. "Except I came home unexpectedly." He munched his cookie. "Since Haleigh is marrying Willie, I guess that means you'll have to marry me," he took another cookie, "so I can have your Christmas cookies."

Jackson's mouth dropped open, and his eyes widened. Katie nearly choked on the cookie she was eating. Her face turned red. She exchanged glances with Jackson, then picked up her mug and took a long drink. Katie had told him that Jesse had a sense of humor. Maybe he was teasing, but something in his voice and earlier handshake gave Jackson the impression he wasn't.

Jackson felt bad for Jesse. He really did. His most serious injury, a sprained ankle from high school gym class, had resulted in a couple days of ice packs and crutches, frustrating enough for an active teen. Jesse faced a longer, harder road to recovery.

Jesse shifted in his chair. He reached over to pull Chloe to his chest. His cheeks and ears red, he didn't look at either of them. "Sorry. I was just ... kidding. You know me. I kid a lot."

Jackson took another cookie. "These cookies are good.

Maybe you girls should go into business together." The tension in the room eased.

Katie shook her head. "I don't think so. If we baked all the time, we'd probably eat all the time, and we'd get fat." She set down her mug. "But you should taste Haleigh's chocolate cake with fudge frosting."

"I remember. She made one for a church dinner once. All I got was a tiny sliver," Jesse whined.

Katie caught his eye. "If you behave, maybe she'll make one for you."

"Oh, I definitely need at least one to help me get better. I'll put in my order for New Year's Day."

Jackson felt like an intruder in a private discussion as he listened to the interplay of words between the other two. He didn't know how to join the conversation. Jesse, wounded in body and spirit, obviously in pain, was not up to having a stranger visit him today. He wished that Katie hadn't invited him to come with her.

Jesse shifted his attention to him. "So, Jackson, how did you meet Katie? You don't live in Greenlawn, do you?"

Jackson looked up. "We had some classes together at college. Now my grandfather's a resident at the Senior Home, and he says she's his favorite nurse."

"What do you do?"

"I'm a middle school history teacher."

"Ah, middle school. Those were the days."

Katie tapped his arm. "If his students are anything like you were, Jess, I'm sure life is pretty exciting for him."

"Oh, Katie, you wound me." Jesse laid his hand over his heart and made a pout. "I was a good student. Okay, I had a few detentions, but nothing serious."

"I have a few stories I could tell. But the kids know I care about them, so they're not too bad, most of the time." Jackson took another cookie and bit into it.

"Is this what you want to do always, or is it a stepping stone to something else?"

"I'll begin grad courses in January to get my master's degree." He glanced at Katie. "For a long time, I've been considering missions, either teaching in a school for *MKs* or going to a mission station on the field." He hadn't shared this information with Katie yet and wondered what she thought.

Jesse finished his hot chocolate and set down the mug. "I'm not sure what I'll do after the Air Force."

"You could be a commercial pilot."

"Maybe, if I can fly again. I thought I'd be so busy right now I wouldn't have time to think about a few years ahead, but here I am with a lot of time on my hands."

"Once you start therapy, Jess, you won't have that spare time," Katie warned.

He groaned. "Don't remind me. I remember Aubrey's therapy after her accident. It took hours out of her day and exhausted her." He grimaced. "I'll find out in a couple of weeks." Jesse yawned.

Chloe sat up. "Mew?"

Katie laughed. "Maybe that's our cue to leave. We're tiring Jesse out."

"Sorry, guys. It's hard to sleep at night. Jackson, before you go, will you help me transfer to my wheelchair? I have to take care of one of life's necessities."

"Sure, what do you want me to do?" Jesse didn't need anything to add to his pain.

With instructions from Katie and Jesse, Jackson assisted Jesse into his wheelchair. "Will you need help when you come back?" he asked.

"If you're willing to wait. Mom can do it, but I know it's hard on her back since I'm so much bigger. So, sure, I can use your help." Jesse wheeled himself slowly down the hallway to the bathroom door. Jackson helped him stand with his crutches and pulled the wheelchair out of the way.

With his hands in his pockets, Jackson sauntered back toward Katie, who sat on the sofa with Chloe in her arms.

He sat next to her. "What kind of accident was Jesse's sister in?"

Katie stroked the cat. "All the Whites are athletic. Aubrey played basketball. During our sophomore year, the girls' basketball team won the state championship. Aubrey's teammate, Leanna Nelson, wanted to take a victory ride with a couple of the guys, so Aubrey went with her. The problem was, the driver of the car had been drinking. He drove recklessly and crashed. Leanna died, and Aubrey was seriously injured." Katie's words stopped.

He touched her shoulder, and she jumped. "Are you all right?" Jackson asked softly.

She sighed. "I'm okay. It was a hard time for all of us." She stood and handed Chloe to him. "I'm going to take the tray out to the kitchen for Mrs. White. I'll be right back." She swept up stray cookie crumbs with her hand, plumped Jesse's pillows, then smiled at Jackson as she picked up the tray and left the room.

He heard the voices of the two women from the kitchen as he scratched the cat behind her ears. He looked at the family pictures hanging on the wall, several portraits of the entire family, individual portraits of the four siblings, and formal wedding portraits of the senior Whites and two of their children.

Jesse opened the bathroom door, and, setting the cat on the floor, Jackson hurried to help the wounded man into his wheelchair and back into the living room. They both burst out laughing at the indignant cat, who sat with her back toward them, swishing her tail.

The women came into the room. "What's going on? What are you laughing about?" Katie looked from Jackson to Jesse.

Jackson pointed at the cat. "Chloe is insulted because I put her down to help Jesse."

"Poor, neglected Chloe." Katie lifted her from the floor.

Jackson helped Jesse get settled in the recliner, then he and Katie prepared to leave.

When he put out his hand, Jesse shook it and said, "Thanks for your help and for your visit."

"Good to meet you, Jesse." He turned to Jesse's mother. "Mrs. White, the hot chocolate and the cookies were delicious. Thank you."

"You're welcome, Jackson. I hope Katie will bring you by again. And I have to confess that I didn't make the cookies. They were a gift." She put her arm around Katie's shoulders.

He nodded. "Katie told us. Thank you for sharing."

Katie gave Mrs. White a hug, and they left with Chloe in her carrier. A light snow fell as they got into the car and drove to the Manns' house.

17

"Thanks for breakfast, Mom." Jackson checked the table and counters for any more dishes. He'd volunteered his brother and sister to help him clean up the kitchen while Mom got ready for her shopping trip.

"You're welcome. You were coming here anyway to pick up Mike and Becky."

"True, but I still appreciate it." When his brother and sister left the kitchen to get their coats, he turned to Mom. "Why didn't you ask Brenda to take the kids today?"

"Brenda's going with me. We planned this shopping trip a while ago. I thought Mike and Becky would enjoy being with you more than going with us."

He and his older sister Brenda were three years apart, but ten and twelve years separated Jackson from his younger brother and sister. Because of the age difference between older and younger children, his parents had two families. He'd often been left in charge of his younger siblings.

"You could have given me more warning. It's a good thing I didn't have plans."

His mother shrugged. "I figured you could work something out. After all, you've been on vacation."

"Mom." He took his mother's coat from her hands. "I love you, and I love my brother and sister. But you have to stop taking me for granted." He tried to keep his voice gentle. "You can't just assume I'll be available every time you need a babysitter."

She bit her lip as Jackson helped her with her coat. "I'm sorry, Jackson. I guess I forget you have your own life now. Thank you for taking them today. They're looking forward to spending time with you and going to see Grandpa Stone."

"And you remember I'm bringing Katie home to meet you when I bring them back?"

She sighed. "Yes, of course. And please plan to stay for supper. I have a pot roast in the slow cooker."

"Is that what smells so good?" He sniffed the air.

"Yes. Dinner will be at six."

"Thanks, Mom." He kissed her cheek. "Well, we'd better go," he said. "I told Katie ten o'clock, and I don't want to be late. Mike! Becky!"

They stopped by the back door to slip on their boots. Glad to see Mike's carefully combed hair and Becky's matching socks, Jackson hurried them out to the car.

KATIE FLITTED ABOUT HER APARTMENT, accomplishing nothing. Jackson had invited her to go to the farm with him to meet his family after their visit with his grandfather.

She put on her new jeans and the green velour tunic, Grandma Whitman's Christmas gift to her, then set out her supply of hot chocolate and Christmas cookies for a snack.

With time to walk to the bank to make her car payment before Jackson arrived with his younger siblings, she donned her outdoor clothing and started out, leaving a zigzag trail in the fresh snow, breathing in crisp winter air, and blowing out clouds of frosty breath.

As she arrived at the bank, Cheryl Nelson Olsen pushed open the door from inside. Her blue coat and matching hat, gloves, and scarf accentuated the blue of her eyes and the glow of her complexion. Her obvious happiness gave Katie joy.

"Hi, Katie!"

"Cheryl, you look wonderful. How are you? I'm sorry I couldn't make it to your wedding."

"I'm just ... wonderful. We're getting settled in as a married couple now. And we're getting ready for the baby."

"When are you due?"

"Early in June."

"Do you know whether you'll have a girl or a boy?"

She shook her head. "I'm having an ultrasound later this month. We're hoping for a healthy baby. I know Lars really wants a boy, but between you and me," she leaned closer, "I'd like a girl. We've chosen a boy's name and a girl's name."

Katie remembered her errand. "I have to make a car payment." She reached for the door, hoping Cheryl didn't think her rude.

Cheryl put a hand on her arm. "I just wanted to thank you."

Katie let go of the door handle and gave Cheryl her attention.

"You took time to be my friend when I needed one. You went out of your way for me. You listened, you prayed, and you shared something very personal with me. And you kept my secret. I know, because the gossip mill hadn't picked up the news before we announced our wedding."

They stepped aside to allow customers in and out of the bank.

Her transparency with Cheryl had paid off. "You're welcome, Cheryl. I'm glad I could help. And I'll be praying for you and Lars and the baby."

"See you in church." Cheryl waved before she turned and walked up the street.

Katie watched her for a moment, then remembered her

errand. She wanted to be back at her apartment before Jackson arrived. The tellers in the bank were all busy, so she stood in line and breathed a prayer of thanks. God had used her own bad choice for good ... ashes to beauty.

BECKY CHATTERED from the back seat about all she'd done during vacation. Mike grumbled from the front passenger seat about having to return to school on Monday.

Jackson agreed with his brother. He loved teaching, but he knew the rest of the school year would be extremely busy, and he wanted more time to spend with Katie.

"Look at it this way, Mike. The sooner you go back to school now, the sooner you'll be out for the summer."

"That's only six months away." Becky looked on the bright side.

"Yeah, right," Mike said.

Becky and Mike discussed classes and classmates. Jackson, grateful for clear roads, tried hard to pay attention to them, but his mind wandered to Katie instead.

He looked forward to introducing Mike and Becky to Katie. In college, he had a couple of girlfriends, but their relationships never got to the *meet my family* stage. With Katie, it was different. He wanted his family to know and accept her. He wanted her to belong in his family, to never be an only child again.

He thought he made appropriate responses when they asked him questions until suddenly he heard, "Are you going to marry her?"

"W-what?" He glanced at Mike's serious face.

"I asked if you were going to marry your girlfriend."

Jackson looked at Becky in the rearview mirror. She grinned at him. He wished he'd been following their conversation a little closer. He waited while the car behind him passed.

"That's kind of a personal question, isn't it?"

Mike shrugged. "Just wondered. We heard Mom and Dad talking the other day."

Should he be worried? "What did they say?"

"They said they expect you to get married soon," Becky said. "And Grandpa Stone talks about her a lot."

How should he respond? He could become angry and tell them it was none of their business. He could say no. After all, he and Katie hadn't approached the subject directly.

"I haven't asked her." He glanced at his brother. "Remember, you're going to meet her in a little while. Katie is really, really nice, and I want you to be nice to her."

"Is she pretty?"

Jackson chuckled at Mike's question. His math teacher from middle school had been fresh out of college, and she had blonde hair pulled back in a ponytail and blue eyes. He thought her to be the smartest, prettiest teacher ever. He imagined his brother would be quite taken with Katie Mann.

"Yes. She's a nurse, and she directs a drama team at her church."

"Does she have brothers and sisters?" Becky asked. "Do you think she'll like us?"

"No brothers or sisters, although she wanted some. She'll like you, I'm sure." Meeting new people was hard for shy, quiet Becky. She usually took a while to warm up to strangers.

They drove into Greenlawn, and Jackson pulled up in front of Katie's apartment house. As he got out of his SUV, she walked out the front door, so pretty in her pink jacket, with her curls cascading over her shoulders. She stopped to pat the snowman on the front lawn.

"Wow!" his brother said.

Jackson grinned.

She smiled at him. "Hi, Jackson. Mr. Snowman is still hale and hearty." She waved at the two kids in the SUV.

"That he is. And you are beautiful as usual." He might have kissed her if they didn't have an audience. Another time.

The color in her cheeks may have been from the cold. "Thank you for asking me to spend the day with you and your brother and sister."

"They're looking forward to meeting my girlfriend. Grandpa always likes to see you, and I'd spend every day with you if I could." Maybe one day.

"Would you, Jackson? I'd like that too."

He opened the car passenger door. Mike wordlessly got out of the front seat and into the back with his sister. Katie slid in, and Jackson shut the door.

Katie turned. "Hi, kids. I'm Katie." She smiled at the silent duo in the back seat as Jackson got in behind the wheel. "You must be Michael. Hi, Michael." She put out her hand, and he shook it. "And you are Rebecca." She shook the girl's hand. "I'm so glad to meet you."

He had to suppress his laughter at their serious, wide-eyed looks. What were they thinking? He hoped they wouldn't embarrass Katie by acting goofy, especially Mike.

"All set?" Jackson looked over his shoulder at his siblings. When they nodded, he turned his attention to Katie. "Are we on time?" He started the car and pulled out on the street.

She checked her watch. "Right on time. We won't stop for Chloe today. I think she needs the day off."

"Who's Chloe?"

Katie smiled over her shoulder at Mike. "She's a therapy cat."

"What's a therapy cat?" Becky leaned forward against her seatbelt.

"Chloe goes with me to the Senior Home to help cheer up the residents there. Some of them miss living at home, and some of them used to have pets of their own. Chloe makes them feel better."

"Oh." They spoke in unison.

"How come we've never seen you when we visit Grandpa?"

"I usually work nights, Michael, so you leave before I get there."

After a short ride, Jackson pulled into the parking lot at the Senior Home. Mike and Becky scooted out of the car. Jackson opened the door for Katie. The two youngsters hurried ahead while Jackson and Katie came more slowly, hand in hand.

"Grandpa's probably waiting for them in the front hall," Jackson said.

Katie took a deep breath. "Do you think I met with their approval?"

Her uncertainty surprised him. "You couldn't tell?" She shook her head. "I watched their faces in the rearview mirror. They're in awe of you."

"Is that good?" she asked.

He squeezed her hand. "Very good."

He opened the door, and she went in. "Oh, by the way, Mom has invited us to stay for dinner. She's having pot roast. Is that all right with you?"

"Of course," Katie said. When he put his arm around her shoulders, she didn't pull away.

Mike and Becky's voices echoed down the hallway as they talked to Grandpa Stone in the common room. Jackson let his arm drop as he entered with Katie. All three looked up. The kids sat on either side of their grandfather.

"Hello, Nurse Katie. Hello, Jackson." Grandpa winked at them. "Two more of my favorite people. We were just talking about you two."

Jackson greeted him with a hug. "Hi, Grandpa. You're one of my favorite people too." His grandfather had recovered well from his stroke.

Katie placed her hands on her hips. "I hope you two didn't tell your grandfather anything bad about us." Mike turned red, and Becky shook her head. Jackson's eyes remained glued on Katie as she leaned over and whispered in Grandpa's ear. "Don't tell any of the other residents, but you're my favorite resident."

She watched Jackson from the corner of her eye, making his heart beat harder and his stomach quiver. Becky shook his arm.

"Jackson, you're not listening to me."

He turned to his sister. "I'm sorry, Becky. What did you say?"

Mike snickered. Jackson's little brother knew where his attention had been, but he had no intention of hiding his feelings for Katie from anyone.

"Will you come sledding with us tomorrow? We both want Katie to come too."

"I don't know, Becky. I have some things to do before school starts next week, and I have to see if I can find the books I need for my college courses on the Internet. If I have the time, maybe."

Katie shook her head. "Thanks for inviting me, Becky, but I can't. I have to work tomorrow. Maybe another time?"

Jackson laid his hand on Becky's shoulder. "There's still time to go sledding. We'll find a day we all have off so we can go, okay?"

Becky sighed. "Okay."

After an hour at the Senior Home, Mike and Becky squirmed in their chairs.

"I think it's time for us to go." Jackson stood.

Mike and Becky quickly shrugged into their coats while he helped Katie put on hers. The kids hugged the elderly man and headed for the door.

"Wait for us by the front door," Jackson called to them. "Don't go out in the parking lot by yourselves." They waved to him in acknowledgment and disappeared into the hall.

"Where's Mary today, Grandpa?"

"She's having her hair done. She said she'd meet me here later."

"Tell her we missed her." Katie kissed his cheek.

"I will. Thanks for stopping by. It's always good to see family." It warmed Jackson's heart that Grandpa included Katie as family.

BEFORE HEADING to the farm in Hope Valley, they ate lunch at the Hillside Diner. Katie had already fallen in love with Jackson's brother and sister. If she married Jackson, she'd have two of her heart's longings fulfilled—she'd have a wonderful husband, and she'd have siblings.

"If you'll stop at my apartment, I can get some cookies to take with us." Katie wanted to take something with her as a peace offering. She'd be meeting Jackson's parents for the first time, and the cookies had been well received by others.

"If they're more of those Christmas cookies, I'm certainly for it." Jackson licked his lips.

When he stopped the car, Katie hopped out. "I'll be just a minute."

"May I come with you?" Becky asked.

Pleased she'd asked, Katie motioned with her hand. "Sure, come on."

The two went into the building and were out again within five minutes. Becky carried a Christmas tin as she got into the back seat. Katie laughed when she saw the girl open the top just a little so her brother could peek in. He licked his lips. She quickly shut the lid and hugged the container.

"Mom and I made Christmas cookies, but Mike ate them up last night," Becky complained.

"You had your share," Mike muttered.

Katie wanted to prevent an argument. "Maybe one day you can help my friend Haleigh and me make cookies."

Becky bounced in her seat. "Really? At your apartment?"

"Maybe. We might be able to use Haleigh's kitchen because she has more room."

"I'd like that."

Thank you, Jackson mouthed to Katie. She nodded.

"Looks like we guys will have to think of something special

to do on that day." Jackson caught his brother's eye in the rearview mirror.

"Cool." Mike grinned.

"All set?" Jackson put the SUV in gear and checked for traffic.

"All set," Katie said, echoed by the other two.

18

"So, you met all of Jackson's immediate family?" Haleigh asked.

Katie nodded and swallowed before answering. "The whole crew."

Aubrey leaned forward. "How was it?"

"Interesting," Katie said, "fun, nerve-wracking, noisy, exciting, exhausting ..."

Aubrey held up her hand, and Haleigh touched Kate's arm. "Okay, okay, we get the picture."

Katie laughed with them.

The Three Sisters had met for raspberry iced tea and chocolate chip cookies at the café, on New Year's Eve afternoon, just like they did when they were kids. Katie listened as Aubrey talked about Jeremy, teaching, and their goals for the future. Haleigh, of course, talked about wedding plans. Now Katie had to answer questions about Jackson.

"Mike and Becky are a blast. By the way, Haleigh, I promised Becky we'd make cookies one day and wondered if we could do it in your kitchen. Your kitchen is bigger than mine."

"Oh?" Haleigh widened her eyes, then smiled. "We'd better

171

do it soon. Time is getting short, you know. Only a little over two months until the wedding."

"We'll set a date." Katie picked cookie crumbs off her plate. "You two know I always wanted to be a member of a big family." They nodded. "Well, I think God has answered my prayers. When I first met Mrs. Stone, she seemed, well, aloof, as though she didn't want me there. But after a while, she warmed up and even gave me a hug when I left. And I have a standing invitation to go back any time."

Aubrey leaned forward. "Is Jackson the one?"

Katie glanced at Haleigh, who rested her chin in her hand, waiting for Katie's answer. Katie nodded. "I think so, Aubrey. He said he'd never go away, and he didn't. Even when I told him about Nathan and the baby." She twisted her tea glass. "My parents like him, even my dad, and Chloe loves him."

"I knew right from the start that Jackson would one day marry Katie. I could tell by the way he looked at her the first time I met him." Haleigh looked smug.

"Like we all knew that my brother would marry you one day." Haleigh made a face at Aubrey. "But I assume Jackson hasn't asked you to marry him yet."

"No, he hasn't asked yet." Katie folded her arms and hunched her shoulders. With a smile, she added, "Maybe soon."

Aubrey leaned back. "And when am I going to meet him?" She had returned to her role as oldest sister, watching out for them. Having Haleigh and Aubrey a significant part of her life again gladdened Katie's heart.

"I have to work the next four nights, but he plans to come to church Sunday, so if you're there, you'll meet him."

"Don't worry. I'll be sure to be there."

Two men standing outside the café peered at them through the window. Katie wished her man was with them.

Katie waved to them. "I think Jeremy and Willie have come looking for you. I guess they're saying the Three Sisters have had enough time."

"We could pretend we've hatched a scheme, although we haven't." Haleigh giggled. "Just to make them worry."

"Let's see if it works." Aubrey got up and pushed in her chair. Katie and Haleigh did the same. They shared a high-five before exiting the café.

They greeted the men, then shared another high-five. Katie left with a smile, heading home to get a few hours of sleep before going to work. She could tell by the questions Jeremy and Willie asked that their plan had worked.

As Katie prepared for church the next morning, she again felt the desire to become a pediatric nurse. As much as she loved the residents at the Senior Home, she wanted to work with children.

Mom had mentioned a temporary opening at the hospital. One of the nurses was going on maternity leave. Did she want to quit her steady job at the Senior Home to take a temporary position at the hospital? Did she want to return to school to get her credentials in pediatric nursing? Both at home and on the mission field, the need was great. She determined to have a conversation with Jackson about it soon.

Jackson had expressed interest in teaching in a mission school. They could work together in a Third World country. Jeremy and Aubrey were looking into the possibility of becoming missionary church planters. Willie and Haleigh would probably be home-front people—prayer warriors and financial supporters.

So much to think about.

Jackson missed church, and Katie could only get his voicemail when she called him after the service. There was no answer at his family's home either, but she left a message. She alternated between worry, frustration, and anger ... then fear. Where was Jackson?

As they moved into the aisle, Aubrey looked toward the church door. "I wonder what happened to him? I'm disappointed. I really wanted to meet him. I'll have to give him a piece of my mind."

"I wanted you to meet Jackson." Katie checked her phone again.

"I remember when you gave me the cold shoulder because I forgot your school play." Jeremy shivered. "I'm glad you forgave me."

"Jackson doesn't seem to be irresponsible." Haleigh shook her head. "He wouldn't stand you up. There has to be a reason he's not here."

Katie gave her friend a grateful look for the words of encouragement.

Willie said, "Why don't we pray? We don't know where Jackson is, but God does."

They formed a prayer circle in the church aisle and prayed for Jackson. Katie thanked them, but she fought fear and hurt as she tried to believe Jackson had a good reason not to be there. Why didn't he at least call or text?

"Come home with us for dinner. We don't want you to eat alone." Aubrey laid a hand on her arm. "We were going to ask you and Jackson anyway, and adding one more person to the mix won't make much difference to Mom. We'll keep praying."

"But I have to work tonight." Katie tried to excuse herself from being with a group. She just wanted to go home and worry. Haleigh and Aubrey each grabbed an arm and walked her to Willie's Floral Creations van.

She sat across from Jesse at the dinner table. She hadn't had her talk with him yet about the way he treated Jackson the day they visited him. But that conversation would have to wait until another time. She didn't talk much to anyone.

Right after dinner, her two friends drove her back to the

church parking lot to get her car. They followed her home to make sure she got there safely. Her heart felt lighter because of their concern and prayers, but she still found it difficult to sleep. Then she overslept and had to hurry to arrive at the Senior Home in time for her shift.

She tried to concentrate on caring for the residents and hide her worry about Jackson, but from the looks cast her way by residents and staff, she knew she hadn't succeeded in hiding her anxiety.

"Is everything all right, Nurse Katie? You're quiet tonight."

Katie couldn't tell David that his grandson was *AWOL*. That would only make him worry. She smiled and patted his arm. "I'm fine, David."

When visiting hours came to an end, she said good night to friends and relatives of the residents as they went out the front door while she stood by the reception desk.

She turned to go back to the common room when the front door opened. Her heart thumped and her breath shortened. A pale and limping Jackson walked in the door, his hair disheveled, dirt stains on his pant legs, but with a smile for her. Katie had to use all her self-control not to rush up to him and throw her arms around him.

She stepped forward. "Are you okay?" Obviously, something was wrong, but her brain wouldn't give her better words.

He leaned against the front desk. "Yes. No. Do you have a moment to talk?"

She turned to the aide standing there. "I'll be in the breakroom if you need me." She raised her hand with five fingers up. The aide nodded with a sympathetic look at Jackson, understanding Katie needed a five-minute break. Katie led Jackson down the hall to the staff break room, grateful that no one else was there. She shut the door.

"Katie, I'm so sorry."

"Sit down before you fall down." She took his arm and guided him to the loveseat.

Jackson sat, letting his head fall back and closing his eyes. Katie brought him a cup of water.

"You look like a truck ran you over." She remained standing after she handed him the cup, wondering if she'd have to call an ambulance for him.

He shook his head. "It was bizarre." He drank some water. "I was on my way to Greenlawn for church. Honest." He raised his hand and looked at her.

She nodded. "I believe you."

He laid his head back. "The road was clear, no ice or snow, but the guy ahead of me in a pickup truck kept swerving and finally ran off the road and hit a tree."

Katie sat down. "Was he okay?"

"I think he hit his head or something. He had a lump on his forehead and seemed dazed when I approached his car. I pulled out my phone and called 911, then I recognized him. That friend of yours, Nathan."

"Nathan West?" She didn't think Nathan drank or used drugs. "Why did he go off the road?"

"I'm not sure. I opened his door to check on him, and he jumped out and punched me in the gut." Jackson rubbed that area. "Then he started to run. But he fell and just lay there."

Katie laid her hand on Jackson's arm.

"I had a blanket in my car, so I did my best to keep him warm until the ambulance and police got there." He took a sip of water. "The police asked me all kinds of questions, and I did my best to answer them. I followed the ambulance to New Hope Hospital. They found his cell phone and called his family, so I waited until they got there. Then they wanted to ask me about the accident."

"Why didn't you call?" Even if he had a good reason to be delayed, he could have called her.

"I dropped my phone when he hit me and didn't realize it until later. I couldn't remember your number because I usually speed dial it. I hoped to get to Greenlawn sooner, but the nurse at the emergency room decided I should have a doctor to look at me, so that took more time."

"Did they find out what happened to Nathan?"

"They wouldn't tell me what caused the accident, but when he learned he'd punched me, he apologized." He reached for her hand. "I came as soon as I could. I went back to the accident site and found my phone and recharged it in my SUV on the way here. But I'm here."

She held his hand between hers. "Jackson, I'm so glad you're all right. I worried when you didn't show up and didn't call."

"I knew you'd do that, and I wish I didn't miss spending the day with you."

She brushed hair away from his forehead and evaluated his condition. "Do you think you can drive home safely tonight?" No, of course not. He was exhausted. "On second thought, why don't you plan to stay with my parents."

"I don't want to bother them."

"I assure you, they would rather you do that than have an accident on your way home."

She called, and her father answered. When she hung up, she said, "They'll be right over to pick you up."

"Okay." Jackson leaned back with a sigh. "I'm glad to finally be here. My family is away until tomorrow night. They couldn't get home until tomorrow anyway, so I told them they should stay and enjoy themselves."

"I have to get back out there." Katie pointed to the door. "Do you prefer to stay in here or come out to the desk to wait for my mom and dad?"

"If you don't mind, I think I'll stay in here. I'll be fine by myself for a few minutes, and I don't want people asking me questions tonight. I'm just too tired." He yawned and smiled. "See?"

Relieved to see his smile, she opened the breakroom door. "Okay. You won't have to wait much longer."

Jackson had been checked out by a doctor at New Hope

Hospital, he'd managed to drive safely to Greenlawn, and he smiled. She'd have to trust that he'd be all right. Her parents should be there any moment, and he'd feel much better after a good night's sleep.

IN THE MORNING, Jackson awoke, his body stiff and sore. It took him a moment to remember he lay in bed in the Manns' guest room. He turned on his back and disturbed a small body lying against his side.

"Mew." Chloe stood and stretched. She walked up along his body and stopped to sniff his chin.

Jackson rubbed his chin. "Silly cat, you're tickling me." He stroked her and she lay down on his chest and began to purr. "Good morning, Chloe." How did she get in?

The small room was furnished simply but comfortably. His clothes lay clean and folded on the chair. Katie's mother washed and dried them for him after he took a shower and put on borrowed pajamas last night. As he lay in bed, he recalled the events of the day before, hardly believing they'd happened but knowing they were true.

Thank you, God, for keeping me safe yesterday and providing this place for me to sleep last night. I pray that Nathan West is all right. Thank you for Katie's presence when I walked into the Senior Home last night, and that she accepted my explanation for being so late. Thank you for Katie and her parents and their hospitality.

He looked at the bedside clock. Katie would be off from work now. He'd better get up. He dressed as Chloe sat on the bed and washed herself. When he opened the door, she glided through and disappeared.

And God, help me to have the courage to tell her parents that I love Katie and want to marry her.

Mr. Mann had laid out shaving supplies for him in the

bathroom. After shaving and combing his hair, Jackson made his bed, folded the borrowed pajamas, and entered the kitchen.

Chloe ignored him as she ate food from her dish. Mr. Mann, tall with dark hair and blue eyes, stood at the stove flipping pancakes while Mrs. Mann, dressed for work, shrugged into her winter coat.

Katie had inherited her mother's slender figure and hair and eye color.

Mrs. Mann noticed him first. "Good morning, Jackson. Are you feeling better this morning?"

"Yes, ma'am, thanks to your hospitality."

"I'm glad we could help you. If you'll excuse me, my shift at the hospital begins in half an hour. I must go." She gave her husband a quick kiss, picked up her bag, and went out the door.

"Are you ready for some pancakes this morning?" Mr. Mann indicated the kitchen table set for three.

As Jackson sat down, his stomach growled. "I am. I didn't realize I was so hungry." He had eaten nothing since a bowl of soup and a sandwich yesterday afternoon.

This wasn't the way he planned to spend his last day of vacation, but he was thankful for time to recover from the strange events of the day before.

"Katie should be here any minute. She went home to shower and change before coming over."

Jackson eyed Katie's father's broad back. He imagined Mr. Mann could be a formidable opponent in the courtroom. Before she arrived, Jackson needed to speak with him.

When he cleared his throat, Katie's father turned around. "Mr. Mann, I ... I ..." *Whew, this was hard!*

The older man took a moment to flip the pancakes on the griddle, then turned back to Jackson, who took a deep breath.

"I love Katie, and I ... want to marry her." Jackson forced himself to look the man in the face, the blue eyes seeming to pierce his soul. "Do I have your permission to ask her when the right time comes?"

Katie's father didn't answer right away. He took his time removing pancakes from the griddle and spooning out the batter for four more. He pulled out a chair and sat down across from Jackson.

"My daughter is a special young woman. She's had some trouble in her past, as you know, but she's a treasure. She deserves a man who will treat her as the treasure she is."

He lowered his eyes and rubbed his hand over the tabletop. "I didn't always do that, Jackson. My work and my clients became more important to me during her growing up years. I failed as a father, and her pregnancy became my wakeup call. God made my failings clear to me then, and I hope Katie will tell you I'm different now, by the grace of God."

Mr. Mann's chest heaved as though he struggled to maintain emotional control.

"I hope never to fail her, Mr. Mann, but I'm not perfect. With God's help, I hope never to betray her trust." It had taken long enough for her to trust him.

Katie's father got up to tend to the pancakes, then sat again.

"Having met you and talked with you and hearing comments about you from others in our church family, I believe you to be a man of integrity and faith. Katie has spoken to me about you. You could have left and never come back after she told you about the baby, but you returned. You drove all the way here after your difficult day yesterday so that she knew you intended to keep your promise to her. You have treated her with respect and care."

A car pulled up outside.

"You have my permission and my blessing. And I'm sure my wife would add hers to mine were she here."

Jackson released the breath he'd been holding. "Thank you, Mr. Mann," were his only words before Katie opened the door. He stood as she entered, energized, his aches forgotten.

Her eyes sparkled, and her beautiful curls lay on her shoulders. Her complexion glowed with the cold.

"Good morning," she said cheerfully. She took off her coat and hung it on a hook by the back door. Rubbing her hands together, she kissed her father's cheek. "Yum, pancakes!" As she turned to Jackson, their gazes connected, and her eyes softened.

He wanted to wrap his arms around her and kiss her. Self-conscious in the presence of her father and out of consideration for Katie's feelings, he knew there would be a better time and place to share their first kiss.

"Good morning, Miss Kate," he said. "Did you have a good night?"

Katie sat next to him, tipped her head, and tapped her lips with her finger. "It was okay for the most part, but there was this weird guy who showed up with a story about a car accident and arriving late for an appointment."

He found her hand under the table and clasped it in his. "Sorry about that. I hope it won't happen again." He shivered when he remembered Nathan's appearance and actions at the scene of the accident, the trip to the hospital, and being questioned by the police. He rubbed his sore midsection where Nathan had punched him.

She nodded. "Me too. I'm glad you're okay. You did a good thing, Jackson. I'm proud to be a friend of a Good Samaritan."

Heat rose up his neck. "I'd want someone to do the same for me."

"Shall we eat?" Mr. Mann came to the table with a stack of steaming golden pancakes on a plate.

"My dad makes the best pancakes," Katie boasted. "Wait 'til you taste them."

19

When Katie's day off coincided with an evening Jackson had free, she and Haleigh prepared a special roast beef dinner and invited Jackson and Willie to eat with them at Haleigh's place. Candlelight and Christian music playing softly in the background added a relaxing and romantic ambiance.

"I understand you're taking graduate courses and coaching a team of honor students for academic competition, Jackson." Willie spread butter on his roll.

"Yes, graduate courses are necessary to get permanent teacher certification, and I'd like to get a master's degree. The school likes each teacher to be involved in an extracurricular activity with students. Coaching the kids is fun and challenging."

"With my work schedule and one night a week taking crisis pregnancy hotline calls, Jackson and I hardly see each other except for church on Sunday." Katie gently nudged Jackson's arm with her elbow.

With the new year, Jackson and Katie had to work around busy schedules to find time together, and giving up time with Jackson was hard. Girls and women had to know the alternatives to abortion and learn that people cared about them and their babies. In the three weeks she'd worked the hotline, Katie had already talked with a young woman contemplating suicide and a young man whose girlfriend didn't want an abortion.

"At Floral Creations, we always know when Haleigh's been taking calls on the hotline. I have to check regularly to be sure she's not asleep on her feet while she's arranging flowers." Willie grinned at Haleigh, and she wrinkled her nose at him.

"When Katie first asked me to be a counselor, I didn't think I could do it," Haleigh said. "But after talking to Katie's grandmother and taking the training, I wanted to do it. It's not easy, and sometimes the calls come in all night long. I'm glad for an understanding boss."

Willie squeezed Haleigh's hand where it rested on the table between them.

"You're seriously considering resigning from your position at the Senior Home to take a temporary position in the pediatric ward of the hospital?" Jackson asked.

His sudden change of topic startled Katie. He hadn't opposed the idea when she first told him. Why did he choose to challenge her in front of friends at a time that should have been relaxed and enjoyable for them?

Katie set down her fork. "Yes. I've applied for the temporary position of pediatric nurse at the hospital. I have to give the Home two weeks' notice, so I have to hand in my letter of resignation by next week."

"You'll be leaving a steady job for a temporary one, right?" Jackson spoke calmly, but she struggled to remain unruffled.

Katie glanced at Haleigh and Willie, who politely concentrated on eating. They already knew she wanted to become a pediatric nurse, and so did Jackson.

"It's not that I dislike working at the Senior Home. I love the residents there. It's just that, well, I want to work in pediatrics rather than geriatrics. This opening is for six months while the regular nurse goes on maternity leave. After that, there may be another opening for me at Greenlawn Community Hospital, or

I'll find a position elsewhere. This will give me some experience, but I'll have to take specific training and courses for my credentials too."

"Grandpa will be disappointed if you leave."

Was he trying to cause an argument? Katie pushed her food around on her plate. The silence was nearly unbearable.

"Katie." Jackson put down his fork and removed the napkin from his lap. "Will you please come to the living room with me? Please excuse us."

Haleigh and Willie looked up and nodded as Katie stood and followed Jackson into the living room. She faced him and crossed her arms in front of her, struggling to keep her temper in check.

"This isn't a sudden or rash decision, Jackson. You know pediatrics has been on my heart for a while. I feel this is an opportunity God has brought my way. I don't want to hurt your grandfather's feelings, but—"

Jackson tugged her arms apart and grasped her hands. He held them against his chest, where she felt his heartbeat. "It's okay, Katie. I'm sorry if I made you think I was against it. I'm trying to process the details, and I want to be sure you're sure." He brushed her cheek with one hand.

Katie nodded, but she focused her gaze down and to the side. Her stomach roiled like river rapids. She'd witnessed quarrels between her parents that had shaken her world, and Jackson's challenge to her decision did the same.

She allowed him to raise her chin with his finger. "I didn't intend for this to become an argument. I just wanted to talk about it. You and Haleigh have put a lot of work into this dinner, and I'm sorry I spoiled it for you. Please forgive me?"

She saw the regret in his eyes. "I forgive you. I don't mind talking about it. It will be a big change for me, and I want your perspective. But why did you challenge me in front of my friends?"

"I didn't mean for it to sound like I question your ability to make a good career decision. It was a mistake for me to speak the way I did." He kissed her fingers. "Let's go back in and finish dinner, okay? We'll talk about this another time. I need to apologize to Haleigh and Will."

"So, it's all right with you that I go ahead with my plans?"

"You're a good nurse, Katie. I can't stand in the way of what God wants you to do. And I want you to be happy."

"Thank you." Her stomach had calmed to an occasional ripple. She didn't have to choose between Jackson and her career.

THE EARLY FEBRUARY thaw left bare, brown lawns and big puddles on the sidewalks. Glad for her waterproof boots as she walked to meet Haleigh for lunch, Katie enjoyed the caress of the sun and breeze on her face. The weather promised spring, making her long for it, although a snowstorm could quickly remove any thoughts of an early spring.

She released a sigh, missing Jackson. She worked days at the hospital now, and this was her first day off since she'd started in pediatrics. Katie didn't regret the change, and she'd learned a lot during her orientation and training. However, the stress of making the change left her tired. A chat with Haleigh would be refreshing.

She entered the café and looked around for her friend. Haleigh waved to her, and Katie made her way between tables and chairs to reach her, greeting nearly everyone there.

"Jesse!" Her squeal made other diners turn their heads. She didn't care.

Jesse stood and clasped her hand, a big grin on his face. He had the cast off his leg, and the bruise on his head had disappeared.

"It's so good to see you. How are you? How is therapy progressing?"

Jesse laughed. "They let me off for good behavior. I'm home

for now, but I have to work on my own for a while to build up my body and continue to heal. Then I'll have to do basic training all over if I pass the physical."

"When he found out you and I planned to meet for lunch, he begged to come. I told him he could only if he behaved himself." Haleigh raised her eyebrows.

Jesse pointed to himself and mouthed, "Me?" with a look of innocence that made Katie and Haleigh both laugh.

"You look good, Jesse." Katie sat and picked up a menu. "I don't know why I'm looking at this. I know what I want."

The young waitress came over and took their orders and the menus. She cast admiring glances Jesse's way. He smiled and winked at her. "How are you, Amelia?" He was definitely on the road to recovery, flirting with girls again.

The girl blushed. "I'm doing well. It's good to see you up and around."

"It's good to be up and around, I assure you."

"I'll bring your lunches in a few minutes." With another look at Jesse, Amelia walked away.

"Amelia's a nice girl," Haleigh said. "I think she enjoys waitressing."

"She likes people." Katie twisted a curl around her index finger. "And I think she has a crush on Jesse."

She hoped Amelia knew Jesse well enough not to take his flirting seriously.

Jesse shrugged. "She's a little too young for me. And I'm not looking for a girl right now." However, if the right young woman appeared, Jesse would probably be more than happy to be friends with her.

Haleigh excused herself to go to the restroom. Alone with Jesse at the table, Katie decided this would be a good time to have a quick heart-to-heart talk with him. Just as she took a breath to speak, Jesse leaned forward and laid his hand on hers.

"I want to apologize to you about the way I treated your

friend Jackson when you brought him to see me at my house." He dropped his gaze and began pushing his silverware around.

"Oh?" She wouldn't have to confront him after all.

"To be perfectly honest, Katie, I-I've cared for you for quite a while." He swallowed. "I fell in love with you, and when I met Jackson and saw the relationship you have, I ... well, I was jealous. I wanted to be in Jackson's place. I wanted you to be my girl."

Katie folded her hands on the table and leaned forward so she could speak for Jesse alone to hear. "I knew there was a problem. I could tell you were challenging him, and so could he. I mean, he never said anything afterward, but I could tell he was uncomfortable. I wondered if I'd have to have a talk with Brother Jesse."

"I figured my bad attitude kept you away. You and Chloe didn't come back for a visit before I started therapy. The only time I saw you was at dinner that day. Jackson's a good guy, and I hope to see him again and get to know him better before I go back." He spun his knife around on the table. "I'm okay with it now, although I'm sorry it couldn't be me."

"I'm sorry if I ever did anything to make you think—"

"No," he said before she could finish, "it was just me. You were always Katie, kind and beautiful and compassionate." He directed his gaze to her face. "I hope he realizes he's won a treasure."

Katie knew her failings. Pleased, yet sobered, by his compliment, she took a deep breath. "You're a very special friend and brother, Jess, although you can be a real pest."

He chuckled and shrugged.

"My heart nearly broke when I heard about your accident. We didn't know the seriousness of your injuries at first. I am so thankful God spared your life. He has a special plan for you and perhaps a special someone. He will lift you up on eagle's wings, and you will fly."

Jesse shook his head. "How do you do that?"

"What?"

"Find Bible verses to fit each situation."

She closed her eyes. "But can't you just feel it, Jess? Think about soaring like an eagle and following God's way." Credit it to her love of drama, but Katie could feel herself lifted by air currents, the wind blowing in her face, her hair billowing out.

When she opened her eyes, Jesse's grin was in place. "Did you have fun flying with the eagles?"

She smoothed her hair and nodded. "I believe God's plan for my future includes Jackson. I want the two of you to be friends, not only because of me but because you're Christian brothers."

With Haleigh returning, Katie held out her hand. "Deal?"

Jesse clasped her hand. "Deal. But if he doesn't treat you right, he'll answer to me."

Katie nodded and let go. "I'm not worried." Jackson would treat her right.

2 0

Not since grade school had Jackson been so excited about Valentine's Day. Back then it was full of school parties with food, games, and exchanging cards with classmates and a special girl. Jackson remembered several times when he held his breath to see if he'd get a *Be My Valentine* greeting from his latest classroom crush.

After trying on three shirts and six ties, he finally settled on a pink shirt with a dark red striped tie. He tried not to be distracted from his driving by thinking about the tiny black box in his pocket, or by the homework papers lying on the table at home waiting to be corrected, or by the reading he had to do for his online course. He kept going over his prepared proposal speech. Everything had to be perfect.

Even the weather cooperated. The quarter moon shone above the empty tree branches. The predicted storm lay miles to the south, the weatherman promising it would bypass Greenlawn.

He pulled up in front of the apartment house and got out of his car, carrying a bud vase with one red rosebud, ferns, and baby's breath. Katie usually met him by the front door, but she had agreed to let him call for her at her apartment door tonight. The curtain in her living room moved, and he hurried inside and up the stairs. The television sounded from the Cases' downstairs apartment, and music drifted from the apartment across the hall from Katie's.

Jackson smoothed back his hair and brushed some specks of lint from his overcoat, then he knocked on Katie's door.

He sucked in his breath when she opened the door. A cranberry-red dress flowed over her feminine figure and reached just below her knees. Her shoes matched the dress. A few curls floated about her face with the rest of her hair pulled into a chignon at the back of her neck. Gold earrings sparkled in the light, and a matching heart pendant lay against her throat.

He handed her the vase. "Katie," he breathed. "You're beautiful!"

She blushed as she smiled and buried her nose in the rose. "Thank you, Jackson."

She stepped back, leaving the door open, and placed the vase on the coffee table. When she lifted her long, black coat from the sofa, he stepped in to help her put it on. A light, sweet fragrance emanated from her hair.

As they reached the bottom of the stairs, a man about Grandpa's age opened his door and stepped out. Had he been waiting for them?

"Well, you young folks have a good time tonight."

Katie looped her arm through Jackson's, sending his heart into high gear. "Thank you, Mr. Case. I'd like you to meet Jackson Stone."

Jackson reached out to shake his hand. "Good to meet you, sir."

"Same here." Mr. Case squinted at Jackson. "You're not the young fellow who bellowed in the hallway at Katie. I almost called the police to take him away." He shook his head. "You take good care of her, son. And have a good time."

"Thank you, Mr. Case. I'll take good care of her and return her safely." Although surprised by the older man's sudden appearance, Jackson felt easier knowing that Katie had someone she could count on right there in the apartment house. He'd been worried after hearing Nathan's tirade over the phone that night.

"Do you and Mrs. Case have any plans for tonight?" Katie asked.

"Not tonight. My sweetie and I decided to let the young folks have the fun tonight. We'll go out another night when things aren't so crowded." He cupped his hand beside his mouth, like a conspirator.

Jackson leaned forward.

"The wife fixed a candlelight dinner for two tonight." Mr. Case winked and smiled before he stepped back into his apartment and shut the door.

Jackson's eyes met Katie's, and they burst into laughter. Mr. Case had set a positive tone for their special evening together.

When Jackson pushed open the outside door, cold air hit them. He shivered, and Katie pulled her coat together at the neck.

He offered her his arm. "Mr. Case is quite a guy, isn't he?"

She curved her gloved hand around his elbow. "The Cases are a sweet, loving couple. They watch out for all of us in the building."

"That's good." He didn't bring up the episode with Nathan because he didn't want to ruin their perfect evening with talk about Katie's former boyfriend.

Jackson had planned the dinner date carefully, choosing a highly recommended but reasonably priced restaurant between Greenlawn and Waverly called the Old Stone Inn. He'd made reservations a month ago. Strings of small, white lights gave the room a romantic glow. Red tablecloths set with white cloth napkins and centerpieces of hearts and roses reflected the Valentine theme.

Katie held his arm as they followed the hostess to their table in a corner of the dining room. A large plant on one side gave them more privacy. *Perfect!*

He could hardly keep his eyes from Katie, and the touch of her hand in his sent waves of electricity through him.

They ordered, and as they waited for their food, Jackson's hand went to his pocket several times, assuring him that the box was still there.

Katie looked around her and sighed. "This is a lovely restaurant, Jackson. I've heard about it but never eaten here."

"Some of my teacher friends have been here and recommended it. I-I wanted tonight to be special."

"It is." Her eyes reflected the light, and he lost himself in her gaze.

A voice intruded on their intimate moment. "I hope I'm not interrupting something important. I saw you guys over here and thought I'd say hello."

Jackson's heart sank as he pulled his eyes away from Katie's. "Hello, Nathan."

Nathan West stood beside their table, dressed in a suit and tie and leaning on a cane, a scar on his cheek. Katie's expression was not welcoming, and he shifted uneasily.

To Jackson, he said, "I wanted to thank you for your help that day when I had the accident. I was kind of out of it and didn't get a chance to talk much to you when I woke up. You saved my life, and I appreciate it." He held out his hand to Jackson.

Jackson glanced at Katie, whose wide eyes registered surprise. He stood and shook hands with Nathan. "I'm glad I came along and could help you. That was quite a day."

"I hit you when you tried to help me." Nathan rubbed the back of his head. "I'm sorry about that, and I'm glad you're okay."

"Thanks." Jackson sat down.

"Are you here with someone tonight?" Katie asked. Jackson had wanted to ask that question, but she beat him to it.

"Derek Hall and I are double-dating with a couple of girls from my church." He pointed to a table in the middle of the dining room, where Derek talked with two young women who looked like sisters.

"Oh, that's nice." Katie glanced at them and smiled.

Jackson relaxed, relieved that Nathan had someone else to hold his attention tonight.

Nathan tapped the tabletop. "Well, maybe we'll meet again. Have a great time, you two. Happy Valentine's Day." He started to walk away, then turned back. "Oh, Katie, I'm sorry I acted like such a jerk. I wish you guys the best."

"Thank you, Nathan." She watched him limp away, then she looked back to Jackson. "Wow! I didn't expect to see him tonight. I'm sorry, Jackson."

He lifted her hand and stroked the back of it with his thumb. "Not your fault." He leaned forward. "I think he was trying to say that he accepts defeat and will leave you alone from now on."

"I hope so." She pushed a curl away from her face. "There's no one for me but you."

When she smiled at him, Jackson focused on her lips, and his heart nearly crashed through his chest. "I hope so too." He had to be satisfied with kissing her hand for now. The waiter brought their dinners, and they soon recovered the intimacy they'd shared before Nathan's appearance.

They finished their meal, and the waiter approached their table. "Would you like dessert? We have several special choices for Valentine's Day."

"Katie?" Jackson looked at her.

She shook her head.

He said, "No, thank you. The dinner was excellent, however. I will be glad to recommend this restaurant to my friends."

"Thank you." The waiter bowed his head to acknowledge the compliment. "I'll bring your check." A minute later, he returned and laid the check folder on the table next to Jackson. "I hope you have a nice evening."

"Thank you," they said in unison as he walked away.

When Jackson moved, Katie lifted her purse and prepared to stand. Instead of standing up, he slid his chair closer to hers, positioning himself so the plant gave him more privacy, and leaned forward. Breathing in her fragrance, he lifted her left hand and looked deeply into her eyes.

She licked her lips. "Jackson?"

"Katie." He stopped, his prepared speech wiped from his mind, "Do you think ... will you marry me?"

Katie opened her mouth and closed it. He held his breath. She lowered her eyes to their clasped hands then raised them to his face.

"I love you, Katie. Please say yes." He tightened his hold on her hand.

She nodded. "Yes. Oh, yes, Jackson," she whispered.

He let out his breath and removed the box from his pocket. She didn't notice it right away. When she did, her mouth formed an *O*. He opened the box.

"Oh, Jackson, it's beautiful!" The gold ring with a small diamond reflected the light around them.

He removed the ring from the box, his hands trembling. It fit perfectly on the ring finger of her left hand. "I hope it's okay." His present finances dictated his choice of rings.

She held up her hand to admire the ring. "It's beautiful. It's perfect." Her eyes shining with tears, she cupped his cheek with her right hand. "I didn't say yes to get a ring. I said yes because I love you. You are God's choice for me, my answer to prayer. Thank you, God."

He couldn't resist this time. Right there in the restaurant, he leaned over and kissed her. After all, it was Valentine's Day.

When they stepped out of the restaurant twenty minutes later, Jackson frowned. Clouds had covered the moon and stars. A cold wind blew.

"I think the weatherman made a mistake. We're in the path of the storm, after all."

Katie leaned into him as they walked to the SUV. "I hope we can make it home before the snow starts."

He hurried their steps so he could get her out of the wind. In the car, with the heater on high, he finally kissed her the way he'd been wanting to for a long time.

21

atie laid her head against the back of the seat and sighed. What a wonderful evening. His proposal hadn't been unexpected. In fact, she'd hoped he would propose to her tonight. Now, when should they get married?

He grasped her left hand with his right as he drove. "Happy?"

"Very." She turned her face toward him. "Are you?" She sat up so she could see his face in the dim light of the SUV's interior.

His mouth curved upward. "Very." He glanced in her direction. "It's starting to snow. The weatherman was wrong."

"At least we don't have far to drive." Driving in this kind of weather wasn't an anomaly where they lived.

The snow became heavier, and Jackson let go of her hand. "I guess I need both hands right now." He eased up on the accelerator to allow the car to slow and turned up the volume on the radio. "Let's see if we can get a weather report."

"Okay." Katie laid both hands in her lap and leaned her head back against the seat, imagining herself in a white gown, meeting Jackson in a tux at the altar.

"Jackson, do you think ... Oh!" The SUV skidded slightly, jerking her from her reverie.

Jackson gained control quickly and slowed down even more. "The road is slick!"

Headlights shone through the swirling snow ahead of them. Fish-tailing tire marks led them to a car that had spun around before coming to rest in the ditch on the opposite side of the road. They could make out the forms of two people in the front seat.

Jackson pulled over and turned on his emergency lights. He left the SUV running as he reached for the handle to open the door. Katie started to open her door. "No," he said, gently grabbing her arm. "Let me check first."

"But I'm a nurse, and they may be hurt."

"True, but you're not dressed to go out in this weather. If you slip and fall ..." He let his voice fade, but she heard the love and concern for her in it. "If they need your help, then we'll see what we can do." He leaned across her to retrieve a flashlight from the glove compartment.

Katie nodded and sat back in her seat as he exited the vehicle, letting in a blast of cold and snow. She shivered and pulled her coat more tightly around her. Jackson slipped and nearly fell as he made his way across the road. She peered through the curtain of snow, praying for his safety and that of the people in the car. She'd seen the results of accidents when she worked in the ER during training.

Jackson bent and leaned against the car when the driver opened his window. She could hear their voices as they talked but not what they said. A light came on in the car, and Katie's heart jumped. A woman knelt on the front seat, reaching back toward two crying children in car seats, one a toddler, the other just a baby.

Katie started to open her door to get out and help, but she stopped when Jackson moved to the back door and opened it. The man in the driver's seat got out and turned to help the woman crawl across the seat, pushing aside the deflated airbags. Jackson reached in and unbuckled the baby, lifting it into his arms. The baby continued to cry until the other man, presumably the father, took it from Jackson. The toddler, however, clung to Jackson's neck when Jackson released him from his car seat and buried his face in Jackson's coat.

They made their way gingerly across the road, slipping a few times. Katie turned in her seat when Jackson opened the back door. The woman slid in first and took the baby from the man. The baby girl stopped crying. The man got in, and Jackson handed him the little boy. The couple murmured to comfort their children as Jackson got behind the wheel.

He blew on his hands and rubbed them together. "What a night!" He turned the heat to full power. "They called 911. The heater in their car doesn't throw out much heat, so I invited them to sit in my SUV until the emergency vehicles get here." He turned on the interior lights.

Katie released her seatbelt so she could talk to the people in the back. "I'm Katie Mann, and I'm a nurse. Are you guys all right?"

"My heart is still thumping." The woman held her hand to her chest.

"We had on our seatbelts, and I'd already slowed down, so I think there are no injuries. We're just frightened." The man rested his chin on the boy's head. "We're glad you came along when you did. We went out tonight, and we had to pick up the kids from their grandparents. We're on our way home. We didn't expect this snow."

The boy tapped the window with his mittened hand. "Snowflakes."

"Yeah, buddy, lots of snow," Jackson responded.

The little boy thumped his chest. "I not Buddy, I Adam."

Jackson held out his hand, the corners of his mouth twitching. "I'm very glad to make your acquaintance, Adam. My name is Jackson." Adam put his small hand in Jackson's large one. Pulling his hand away, he grinned and leaned back against his father.

"I'm Len Wright, and this is my wife Mae and our baby Brittany. And, of course, our son, Adam," the father said.

Katie smiled at Brittany, who played peekaboo with her. Katie's heart constricted at the little girl's smile.

"Is there anything you'd like me to check?" Katie looked from one to the next, trying to evaluate their condition in the dim light. "Any bumps or bruises?"

"I think we're all okay. The kids were in their car seats. It was astonishing when the airbags inflated." Mae talked with nervous animation, gesturing with her free hand.

Len grasped his wife's hand. "I'm glad we stayed right side up. I almost saw my life flash before me as we spun around."

"Right side up, upside down," Adam chanted. "Upside, inside, outside, down."

"Sounds like a Dr. Seuss book I used to like," Jackson said.

Mae touched her son's cheek. "He loves words and tries to say everything he hears."

Katie hadn't met the Wright family before tonight. "Do you live in Greenlawn?"

Len nodded. "Not right in town. We bought a house up past the shopping mall. I'm the new manager of Dunn's Department Store."

Katie smiled. "I have a long shopping history with Dunn's." She'd shopped there often with Haleigh and Aubrey. "If you live long in Greenlawn, it becomes one of life's staples."

The couple relaxed, and everyone seemed to be okay. Brittany fell asleep in her mother's arms.

Flashing lights appeared from the direction of Greenlawn.

Adam pulled himself forward in his father's lap and looked out the windshield. "Firetruck," he shouted as a county sheriff's SUV and an ambulance slowed and stopped on the opposite side of the road.

"You stay here with the kids, Mae." Len leaned over and gave her a peck on the cheek. He opened the door, got out, and set his son on the seat. "You take care of your mommy and sister, okay, Adam?" The little boy nodded.

"I'll go with Len." Jackson kissed Katie's cheek. Katie blushed on the outside and glowed on the inside.

"Are you two married?" Mae asked.

"Not yet. He just asked me tonight." She pulled off her left glove to show off the diamond.

"Oh, congratulations! How wonderful." Mae leaned forward to examine the ring. "It's lovely. A pretty setting."

"Thank you. I think so." Katie held her hand up to admire the ring.

"I'm sorry we interrupted your romantic evening, but I am so thankful you two came along when you did."

"So am I." Katie wiggled Adam's booted foot that stuck out in front of him. "When we started out tonight, the sky was clear, and the moon was shining. The storm was supposed to go south of us. I wonder how much snow we'll get." The flakes still fell steadily, although more lightly. "Do you like to play in the snow, Adam?"

Adam nodded, his eyes fastened on the men talking to the uniformed emergency responders across the road. They examined the tire tracks in the snow, the car, and its position. The policeman wrote in his notebook. A tow truck arrived, stopped, and backed up to the Wrights' car, while Jackson helped Len remove the car seats. An EMT and the deputy walked over to Jackson's SUV. Adam's eyes grew big when the policeman opened the door and leaned in.

"Is everyone okay?" He looked at each one of them. "Hello, Katie. It looks like you've been out celebrating Valentine's Day."

Reg, the sheriff's deputy, was a familiar face around Greenlawn, and Katie smiled at him.

"Hi, Reg. Not exactly the best way to end it. Where did this snow come from?"

Mae put her arm around her son. "We seem to be fine, officer. Just a little shaken up."

"Why don't you have the EMTs check you out." It wasn't a question. "They'll pull the ambulance right over here." Just then, the ambulance did a U-turn and pulled up behind them.

"That's a good idea, Mae," Katie urged. "I'll go with you if you want."

"No, we'll be fine. Let the nice policeman help you out, Adam." The little boy obeyed, and Mae followed with Brittany.

Jackson leaned into the SUV to install the kids' car seats. "Len asked us to give his family a ride home. No one seems to be hurt."

"Is everything okay, Jackson? I feel kind of helpless just sitting here."

"Just think of me as your knight in shining armor." He grunted as he positioned the seats and buckled them in.

She watched him. "You're getting practice for the future."

"Yeah, I guess I am." The seatbelt clicked, and he wiggled the car seat. "How many do you want, Katie?"

"Car seats or children?"

He looked up at her, his eyes brimming with good humor. "I meant children." He threaded the seatbelt through the bottom of the second car seat.

"Oh, about a dozen." She pretended to watch the tow truck pull the car out of the snowbank as she peered at him from the corner of her eye.

"What?" He jerked backward.

When she saw his open mouth, she burst out laughing. He shrugged and laughed with her.

"I'd like a big family, Jackson. Being an only child myself, I'd like at least two."

He nodded. "I guess we'll have time to talk about it." He jiggled the seats. "That about does it. The policeman will check them to make sure they're in right. Len will ride with the tow truck to the service station. We'll bring the rest of the family. I'm glad I have a big vehicle."

"Me too." As she turned in her seat and fastened her seatbelt, she shivered.

"Sorry, I'm letting in the cold air." Jackson backed out and closed the door.

A few minutes later, the tow truck and ambulance pulled away. Mae and the children got into the SUV with Jackson and Katie, and the police car followed them into Greenlawn.

Bright sunshine and warm air heralded the March wedding of Haleigh Abbott and Willie White.

Haleigh peered into the mirror one more time as Katie waited with her for her father to escort her. Her white satin, A-line gown with a lace bodice overlay and long, lace sleeves fit her petite figure to perfection. Haleigh had made it herself.

"I can hardly believe this day is here. And no snowstorm. I'd rather put up with a little mud than with three-foot snowdrifts."

Outdoors, cheerful crocuses bloomed, and daffodils poked their green spikes through the bare brown soil left behind by melting snow, along with a few small patches of green grass. Indoors, warmth, love, and laughter permeated the air. Once again, the Abbott and White families came together to celebrate love and the beginning of a new family.

"Haleigh, you're the perfect bride. Your gown is beautiful, and your face is glowing."

"I'm not perfect, as you know, but with God's help I'll be the perfect wife for Willie."

As maid of honor for her dear friend, Katie stood within the inner circle of the celebration, and today she didn't want to be elsewhere. Her hunter green, A-line, satin gown matched those of the other bridesmaids, except hers had a lace overlay on the bodice. Her bouquet and all the wedding flowers had been arranged by Willie. Katie loved dressing up for this extra-special occasion.

"I saw Grandpa White come in a few minutes ago. I wonder what words of wisdom he'll have for you and Willie." Katie had first learned of Grandpa White's sense of humor early in life, when she'd spent time with the White family.

"Whatever he has to say to us, I'm sure it will be memorable." The old man knew he could get Haleigh to blush easily, although he never said anything bad or questionable.

A knock at the door stopped their giggles. Katie opened the door and stepped aside. Haleigh's father came in.

"I see you're ready, Haleigh. And you are beautiful."

Katie nodded to Haleigh and stepped out of the room to give father and daughter a moment together.

The strains of "Jesu, Joy of Man's Desiring" sounded from the organ, and the wedding party proceeded down the church aisle. Katie reached the front and turned as the music changed to "Trumpet Voluntary," played by three of Jeremy's seminary friends.

Young Timmy Morgan, Haleigh's neighbor, stood straight and solemn, holding the pillow with the rings. Pastor and Amy's daughter Eve, the flower girl, twisted from side to side in her sage green cotton and lace gown. Jesse, the best man, winked at Katie from his position beside Willie. Mike White and Haleigh's brothers also stood up with Willie. Aubrey, Haleigh's sister-in-law Carmella, and Timmy's mother Nancy were bridesmaids.

Katie's heart overflowed with joy as Haleigh walked down the aisle on her father's arm.

Willie didn't take his eyes off Haleigh as she walked toward him. He mouthed the words *I love you* to her when she reached the front of the church.

Katie shivered. In a few months, she and Jackson would be

standing there. Today, her fiancé sat with her parents near the back on the bride's side of the church.

The music ended, and Pastor Pete's voice brought Katie's attention to the bride and groom and the marriage ceremony.

KATIE AND AUBREY stood outside the door of the room where Haleigh changed out of her wedding gown. Katie knocked. "Haleigh, it's us. May we come in?"

Mrs. Abbott opened the door. "Come in, girls." She put an arm around each one of them. "I'm glad you girls settled your differences. It's so good to have the Three Sisters back." She kissed her daughter. "Don't be long. Willie will be waiting for you." She left and closed the door.

Haleigh now wore a street-length, soft pink dress. Her bridal gown hung on a hook on the wall. "I can hardly believe this day is here, and I'm now Haleigh White instead of Haleigh Abbott."

"We've all waited a long time for today to happen." Katie ran her fingers down the soft, smooth satin of the bridal gown.

Aubrey laid her hand on Katie's arm. "Two down, one to go."

"We'll get busy on your wedding plans when I get back." Haleigh looked around her before closing her overnight bag.

"Jackson and I will have a definite date by then, but it will probably be mid-July. Mom and I have been working on some details. You two will be my attendants, right?"

Haleigh gave her a hug. "Of course."

Aubrey took a deep breath and bit her lip. "Well ..."

Katie, the nurse, for the first time, noticed a translucent quality in Aubrey's complexion. Then her eyes traveled to her friend's midsection. "Aubrey, are you ...?"

Aubrey nodded.

"... pregnant?" Haleigh finished.

They held hands in a circle and jumped up and down and hugged each other.

"We didn't want to say anything to take away from your day, Haleigh. You two are the first to know. We'll tell our families later, though you can tell Willie, Haleigh." Aubrey lifted Katie's left hand and touched the diamond ring. "I'd love to be a bridesmaid. If I can fit into a dress by then."

"Good." Katie laid a hand over Aubrey's. "We'll find a style that will work for you."

Haleigh's mother knocked on the door. "Haleigh, Willie is waiting."

"Okay, Mom, I'll be right out."

"God is so good." Katie pulled the other two into a circle. "He gave us a second chance with our friendship."

"What I would have missed if I hadn't returned to Greenlawn last spring." Haleigh fingered her wedding band. "God showed me how self-centered I'd been. You don't know how much it means to me that you forgave me, and we're friends again."

Katie carefully wiped the tears from her eyes. "No matter where God leads us in the future, we're Three Sisters who love, support, and pray for each other."

They high-fived before Aubrey opened the door.

Willie, Jeremy, and Jackson stood together, leaning against the wall. Willie shook his head. "Do you think it's safe that the Three Sisters are back, Jeremy?"

"We'll have to tell Jackson the dangers after you get back from your honeymoon, Willie."

"Are they dangerous?" Jackson pushed himself away from the wall.

His smile still took Katie's breath away. She shrugged and held out her hand. Together they followed the newlyweds outside to the parking lot, where a crowd of people stood with birdseed to throw, and Willie's highly decorated van stood waiting.

"We're next," Katie whispered.

Jackson pulled her close. "It can't happen too soon."

ABOUT THE AUTHOR

Beth began her writing career in second grade when her poem about her lamb appeared in the school newspaper. With an early love for books and reading, writing for children was her first passion. She writes stories for her grandchildren for their birthdays.

Beth has written articles for church newsletters, ventriloquist routines for her husband, church programs, devotions, puppet scripts, short stories and articles for children, Bible studies for women, and Bible lessons for children.

She earned a B.A. in English from Hartwick College, an ETTA certificate from Practical Bible Training School, a diploma from the Child Evangelism Fellowship Training Institute, obtained training with a crisis pregnancy ministry, and took a course in biblical counseling through a local church. Completing the basic course with the Institute of Children's Literature in 1992, set her on a path to learn to write well and seek publication. She attends Montrose Christian Writers

Conference and is presently a member of a local writing/critique group.

A home missionary with Child Evangelism Fellowship from 1979 to 1984, she. assisted her husband as a Good News Club teacher and teacher trainer. As a pastor's wife for 33 years, she taught children, teens, and adult women and has been involved in music ministry. She became a 4-H leader for eight years, when her children belonged to 4-H, and homeschooled her three children for 12 years.

Some of Beth's holiday manuscripts appeared in Lillenas Drama's *Program Builders,* several devotions in *Penned from the Heart,* and one in *The Secret Place.* "Sadie and the Princess," a short story for preteens, is included in *Heart-warming Horse Stories.* Three contemporary Christian romance novels, *Meadow Song, Heart's Desire,* and *A Heart's Journey* have been published by Scrivenings Press. *Her Heart's Longing* is the third book in The Three Sisters series.

ALSO BY BETH E. WESTCOTT

Heart's Desire

The Three Sisters - Book One

When Aubrey White and Jeremy Abbot meet again at her brother's wedding, neither of them is thinking about falling in love. Both focused on their education and careers, they are surprised by love, and they soon learn that falling in love doesn't follow a straight path to happily ever after.

The stress caused by busy schedules, misunderstandings, a broken promise, a sister's stubbornness, and a secret, threaten to uproot their plans for a future together.

Is God showing them that the desire of their hearts is not His plan for them?

Get your copy here:

https://scrivenings.link/heartsdesire

A Heart's Journey

The Three Sisters - Book Two

Haleigh Abbot returns to Greenlawn, her childhood home, seeking forgiveness and renewed friendships. Willie White hires her to work in his florist shop. Drawn to Willie by his kindness, strength, and faith, Haleigh refuses to allow their relationship to go beyond friendship. Although forgiven and accepted back into the Greenlawn community, shadows of fear and guilt from the past still cling to her. When a little boy and his dog under her care are hurt in a terrible accident, she goes into an emotional tailspin.

Haleigh has held a special place in Willie's heart since childhood. When she left Greenlawn and shut him out of her life, it hurt, but he never forgot her. Her return gives him an opportunity to win her heart. He's ready to help her, but will her determination to prove she can handle life's challenges on her own stand in his way?

Get your copy here:

https://scrivenings.link/aheartsjourney

Meadow Song

Artist Kate Greenway escapes her home town after the death of her finance. She finds a meadow to paint in, a young girl, and the girl's handsome uncle Jack Chambers, and begins to move forward in her life. When Kate's mother develops cancer, Kate has to return home to care for her. Jack cannot make a commitment. She tells Jack the Master Potter can create something new out of the broken pieces of their lives.

Get your copy here:

https://scrivenings.link/meadowsong

Love's True Calling

by Lori DeJong

After years of jumping through other people's hoops to be all they thought she should be, and enduring a tragedy no mother should, self-described "newbie" Christian, Harper Townsend, has finally found her true calling ... and her true love. Until it appears that to follow one may mean leaving the other behind.

Adolescent Psychologist, Wyatt McCowan, is beyond delighted to have *the-girl-who-got-away* back in his life—and his heart. But even as they fall more in love, he realizes that being obedient to God's calling on each of their lives may pull them apart. She rejected him once in favor of another, which left him hurt and angry. But this time, he can't fault her for following hard after the God she loves with all her heart, even if it means leaving him once again.

Get your copy here:

https://scrivenings.link/lovestruecalling

Operation Find a ~~Job~~ Guy

by Amy R. Anguish

Skye Jones has one goal for the summer—keep her father from taking away her convertible. That's the *only* reason she agrees to work at her sister's bridal shop in Boulder, Colorado, while she searches for a non-boring job. Why else would she have anything to do with weddings when she has no interest in marriage?

Benjamin Smith somehow ended up as a groomsman in two weddings over the summer, so he's spending a lot of time at Happily Ever After events. Falling for a blonde with no dreams of settling down wasn't in his five-year plan, yet the more he sees Skye, the more he wants to figure her out.

But all she sees him as is a boring attorney-her complete opposite.

Besides, romance is supposed to be for Skye's friends, not her. And she's in Colorado to get a job, not a guy. Right?

Get your copy here:

https://scrivenings.link/operationfindaguy

Stay up-to-date on your favorite books and authors with our free e-newsletters.

ScriveningsPress.com